"You and I are going to have a He walked across the room and unfolded a camp chair. Opening it, he pulled it over next to the bed on which Joyce lay handcuffed to the bedpost.

Instinctively, with her free hand, she pulled the blanket up in an effort to cover herself. "I don't know anything," she said.

The First Threat

Santino laughed and it wasn't a pleasant laugh. Leaning over suddenly, he took one end of the blanket and jerked it off the bed.

"You got a pretty face," he said. "Pretty face and a nice body. I can spoil them for you. I can turn that face into something that nobody will ever want to look at again. I can do things to that body of yours . . ."

Hostage for a Hood

by Lionel White

WILDSIDE PRESS

To Karl and Mickey Walter

All rights reserved, including the right to reproduce this book or portions thereof.

All characters in this book are fictional and any resemblance to persons living or dead is purely coincidental.

1.

THE ACCIDENT took place at exactly fourteen minutes after nine on Monday morning at a blind intersection where Elm Road crossed Main Street at an oblique angle. It involved two automobiles, one a seven-year-old black sedan and the other a brand-new two-toned job, stolen at daybreak from in front of a doctor's office over in the residential section of the town. The seven-year-old sedan had all of the best of it.

The accident also involved two men, a woman and a medium-sized French poodle. No one was injured, except possibly in spirit, and there were no witnesses. The woman was at fault.

Both drivers were sober and neither was speeding at the time. Material damage was well under a hundred dollars. There was no other property damage. But for a completely insignificant, everyday run-of-the-mill accident, the repercussions were fantastic.

Detective Lieutenant Martin Parks, normally in charge of homicide, but a policeman who kept in touch with almost every activity of the small but efficient Brookside force, would be and was the first to admit this. The lieutenant was not a man given to superlatives or overstatement.

Joyce Sherwood was the woman involved. She had been driving the black sedan. A split second before the crash, she realized what was about to happen. Simultaneously with the realization, she knew herself to be at fault. But she was given no time for idle reflection, and even as she instinctively jammed down on the brake and opened her mouth in the beginning of a small scream, there was a rending crunch of metal against metal and the accident was an accomplished fact.

The impact wasn't great, but it was sufficient to throw the poodle from the seat of the sedan to the floor, where it crouched in hurt, shocked surprise. Joyce herself was shaken up and bruised when her slender, small body rammed forward against the steering wheel. But even in that initial moment of shock, she instinctively reached for the brown suede leather bag at her side which contained the cashier's check for twenty-six hundred dollars. It was the check—which she had obtained only minutes before from the teller at the County Trust Company—which was responsible for taking her mind off of her driving and was indirectly responsible for the accident.

There were no witnesses because the intersection was deserted at the moment and the sound of the crash was not sufficiently loud to attract attention from a distance.

As is usual in such cases, there was a moment of utter silence after the two cars made contact. And then the poodle recovered his vocal cords, if not his dignity, and set up a howl. This served to unblock Joyce's temporary mental paralysis and she reached for the handle of the door at her side. As she started to twist it she saw the doors of the other car open and the two men step to the ground. They moved toward the front to survey the damage.

They were wearing police uniforms, and Joy experienced an odd sense of relief as her mind went to the certified check made out to cash. It was the last time she was to enjoy that particular sensation for a long, long while . . . .

Monday morning.

The bed was a warm, soft refuge and she hated the thought of getting out of it, of getting up and starting the new day.

Actually, the day, for her, had already started, even though her eyes kept closing and she wanted to snuggle up against the firmness of his lean, slender body and fall back into sleep once more.

He of course had done exactly that. Fallen asleep again

almost at once, still holding her tight in his arms, still breathing heavily. He always did, and she always envied him for it, but it was an envy without irritation or jealousy. This was a very special morning and she would have liked to make an exception of it and join him in sleep and just ignore the clock on the side table next to the bed.

A very special day. The first anniversary of their marriage. It always struck her as odd, and a sort of lucky coincidence, that they had been married exactly one day before his birth date. It was thinking of this that suddenly brought her eyes open and alert again. Today it wasn't just a case of disentangling herself from his arms and getting up to prepare the quick breakfast they had together each morning before she drove him to the train. Today she herself had something very, very important to do. Something which she had been planning now for weeks and something which wouldn't wait.

She smiled to herself as she thought about it. And then she moved, hating to do so, slipping away from his arms and sliding over and letting her long, beautiful legs slip off the edge of the bed until her feet touched the floor. A moment later, as she leaned beside the bed reaching for the bathrobe, she saw that he had opened one eye and was looking at her. He half reached out a hand to pull her back to him once more, but she quickly laughed and stepped away.

It was always like this in the mornings; he wanted her then more than ever and she was only too glad to give herself. But this wasn't a weekend and there were things to be done. A lot of things.

Five minutes later she had made her hasty toilet and was back in the bedroom of the apartment, tossing on her clothes with a sort of careless efficiency. She reached down and took a corner of the sheet and quickly tore it off the bed, leaving him lying there naked and exposed, a bellow of false rage already on his lips.

"Come on, Bart," she said. "Get up, boy. You've had it." She laughed, running for the door. "Breakfast in exactly twelve minutes," she called over her shoulder. "You've got a train to make, my friend."

He groaned, rolled over and slowly sat up on the edge of the bed. He was smiling sleepily. He was very happy, very contented, even if he did hate the thought of the train which took him away from her.

He hummed to himself, a series of muted notes, off key, as he shaved, thinking of the things he had to do, the work down at the office which was waiting for him. The job was fine and he liked it. He was young and he worked hard and he was getting places. He just wished that he could get there a little bit faster. There were so so many damned things he wanted; bigger responsibilities, more money. Money to buy things for her. A house of their own which they both dreamed about, out just a bit farther from the city and with a bit of land around it. The new car to replace the seven-year-old sedan which she used to drive him to the station (although he had to admit that the new car was something he wanted more for himself than for her—she was satisfied with the old Chevy.) Furniture, clothes, money for the children which they both wanted and planned on having.

He grimaced, having knicked his chin with the razor, and quickly washed off the remaining shaving cream with cold water. Well, anyway, they would be stepping out on the town tomorrow. It was going to be *his* birthday present to *her;* the tickets to the hit show, the dinner in town and the nightclub and dancing after the play. He'd arrange for the tickets as soon as he got into the office. That was one of the nicer parts about working for Markson Advertising. He was in a spot where he could get tickets for the top hits without giving up an arm and a leg.

She had the two soft-boiled eggs, the buttered toast and the steaming pot of coffee ready when he came into the dining alcove off the kitchen, still lacing his tie around his neck and jerking it into position. He didn't take the glass of fresh orange juice she was holding out, but instead reached for her, lifting her off of her feet and pulling her slender body close as he kissed her lips.

She shook herself free, almost spilling the juice.

"What's got into you?" She laughed. "I guess I'll have to cut down on your feed."

She stepped nimbly around the table, seated herself, and started to fill the two coffee cups.

"You'll have to step on it, my boy," she said, "if you expect to make that train."

"I'll make it all right, honey," he said. "This business of working certainly interferes with a man's pleasure, though."

Twenty minutes later she ran down and opened the garage doors.

Flick, the black poodle, barked wildly, scurrying around her feet for a minute or two, and then rushed out and found his usual fire hydrant. By the time she had climbed into the car behind the steering wheel, the dog had returned and leaped into the back seat. Bart joined her a moment later, having taken a minute or so to find his briefcase.

She backed out of the garage into the street, swung the wheel and put the car into forward, clashing the gears as they meshed. There was no time to get out and close the garage doors.

She had a moment's worry, knowing that she wouldn't be returning directly, as she usually did. But she shrugged and dismissed the thought. It wouldn't matter; there was nothing in the garage of value. Everything she had of value was sitting there next to her on the front seat of the old car, waiting to join a few hundred other commuters on their way to Manhattan on the eight thirty-five.

The lieutenant had missed his supper. Actually, except for periodic containers of coffee which had been brought in to him through the day, he'd had nothing at all to eat since his breakfast at eight-thirty that same Monday morning—and it was now well past ten o'clock in the evening. This was, however, merely a contributing factor as far as his annoyance was concerned.

It had been a highly unusual day in more respects than one; otherwise, he would not have been in his tiny office on the second floor of the combined police station and town hall this late. Also he wouldn't have barked at Coogins—Patrolman First Class Clarence Coogins—when the man came in to tell him that the young fellow was still hanging around waiting to talk with him.

The lieutenant looked up, impatience and irritation reflected in his shadowed, tired eyes. He ran a lean, hard hand through his short-cropped iron-gray hair and with the other hand pushed away the telephone into which he had been speaking. He made a conscientious effort to keep the annoyance out of his voice.

"Okay, Coogins. What is it now?"

"It's this Sherwood fellow—he's still here. Insists on seeing you. I tried to tell him . . ."

The lieutenant sighed. "All right, all right, send him in. But I should think you guys downstairs could handle these routine jobs. I have enough on my mind . . ."

Coogins mumbled something and turned quickly to the door. He'd been on the force for thirty-five years and could well remember when Marty Parks had been assigned to him as a rookie patrolman more than two decades ago. But things had changed—and now he looked on the other man not only with understanding but also with a certain degree of fearful respect.

The lieutenant shuffled through the papers lying on the scarred oak desk in front of him until he found the slip which Coogins had left for him the first time he'd been in about the matter. He adjusted his reading glasses, pulling them down from where they rested on his forehead.

Bartwell Sherwood, 97 Olive Drive. Wife, Joyce Sherwood, missing.

He put the slip of paper back on the desk as the door opened and a painfully slender, rather carelessly dressed man in his late twenties entered the room.

Lieutenant Parks quite unconsciously took in the heavy, horn-rimmed spectacles, the brown, slightly curly hair cut crew fashion, the long, sensitive hands. He catalogued him immediately: Junior executive, undoubtedly a commuter, and a half of one of those young married teams who had been flocking out into the suburbs during the last few years. A young man with a very obviously serious problem on his mind.

Bart Sherwood didn't bother to take the stiff-backed chair which Parks indicated, but stood straight and tense in front of the desk. His spare, rectangular face was pale and he nervously fingered the dead pipe in his hands. The blue eyes under the wide, high forehead were worried and the lieutenant at once realized that whatever the problem was, it was vital, at least to Sherwood himself.

"I am absolutely sure something has happened to her," Sherwood said. "Absolutely sure. You have to do something."

"I've got to do a lot of things," Detective Lieutenant Parks said, his mind still on that other and far more important matter. "Good Lord, I've got . . ." and then quickly he stopped, remembering that after all this thing was a police matter, at least for the moment, and that the man standing in front of him was a resident of the town and a taxpayer and without doubt considered his particular difficulty all-important.

"I'm sorry," he said, interrupting himself. "It's been one of those days. Perhaps you better tell me what it's all about. I understand your wife is missing." He looked down again for a second at the scribbled note. "You're Bartwell Sherwood, and you have reported your wife, Joyce Sherwood, missing. Is that right?"

"Exactly," Sherwood said. "I came home and . . ."

"Came home from where—and when?"

"I work in New York. Copy writer with the Markson Advertising Agency. Joyce—that is, Mrs. Sherwood—drove me to the station this morning; I get the eight thirty-five. She left me as the train was coming in and I went to work. I called her early this afternoon about theater tickets I was planning to pick up. Tomorrow's my birthday," he added irrelevantly, "and I was trying to get seats to a Broadway show, and . . ."

"You called her, and—"

"I called her and there was no answer. That was around two o'clock. And then I called back after half an hour or so. She could have been out shopping. Well, I didn't get her on the second call and so I kept on phoning throughout the rest of the afternoon. I never did get her. I was worried because I knew she was expecting my call—about the tickets, you know. Anyway, instead of taking the usual five o'clock commuter's special, I got a train at four thirty-two. Got me here into Brookside at a few minutes after five-twenty. I grabbed a cab at the station and went directly home. I don't know why, but I was worried."

"Any special reason to be worried?"

"As I told you, I'd been telephoning . . . ."

Lieutenant Parks waved his hand. "Yes—yes, of course," he said.

Bart Sherwood looked at the police officer and frowned. "I got home and the house was locked. The car was gone. I let myself in. The breakfast dishes were still on the table, and as near as I could tell Joyce had never returned after dropping me at the station this morning."

"Why else, aside from the breakfast dishes, did you think she hadn't returned?"

"Well, actually, the breakfast dishes, being left there all day unwashed, would have been enough. Joy is a neat housekeeper. Anyway, I started looking around and the only clothes of hers which seemed to be missing were the ones she was wearing when she'd driven me to the station. The milk, which is delivered around ten in the morning, was still sitting on the back porch. Another thing—the garage doors were open."

"Yes?"

"We're always in a hurry in the morning. To catch the train, you know. So Joy leaves them open, but the minute she gets back—she always goes directly home even if she has shopping to do later—the minute she gets back she closes them, and if she goes out later, for any length of time, she keeps them locked. So I don't think she ever got back from the station."

"Where do you think she went, then?"

Sherwood shifted on his feet and put the dead pipe in his mouth. His expression was half puzzled and half annoyed.

"That's what I'm trying to find out from you people," he said. "I looked around the house and then I started calling up a few friends where she might possibly be. No one had seen her. By seven o'clock I was really worried. I called the local hospitals and the police station, checking to see if there could have been an accident. There was nothing. I made several other calls and then I came down here, around nine o'clock. I reported her missing to the man downstairs on the desk. I can't say he seemed very interested."

"We're always interested when someone turns up missing," Lieutenant Parks said. "Let me ask you a couple of questions. We want to help you all we can, so think carefully about your answers. How long have you been married? Do you have any children? Do you have anyone else living with you? Relatives or anything?"

Bart shook his head.

"There's just the two of us. We've been married exactly one year today."

"Mrs. Sherwood ever leave you before?"

Sherwood shook his head, frowning. "She hasn't left me now. She's missing, I tell you. Something must have happened to her."

Lieutenant Parks nodded.

"You have any arguments recently? Maybe some sort of little tiff this morning, perhaps?"

"Good Lord, no. I tell you there was nothing—nothing at all wrong. Why, we were talking about the celebration tomorrow night and about my getting the tickets to the show. There was no argument at all. We never argue."

"Never? You mean to tell me you've been married a year and you never . . . "

"Listen, Officer," Bart said. "Of course we argue sometimes. But never anything serious. Never anything serious at all. Everybody disagrees now and then with everybody else, but I tell you . . ."

"What was your last argument about?"

Sherwood looked at the other man and his eyes were dark with anger.

"What does it matter?" he asked. "If you must know, it wasn't really an argument at all. I wanted to get a new car, and Joyce thought we should keep the money and save it toward the down payment on a house. I didn't want her driving that seven-year-old heap, but's she's a lot more sensible than I am and she was right. It wasn't really an argument at all."

"All right, all right, you didn't have any serious argument. We have to find these things out, you know. Does your wife have any family, or very close friends whom she might suddenly decided to visit? Maybe someone without a phone?"

"No family. Her folks are dead and she was an only child. I've called all her friends. But she simply wouldn't . . ."

Lieutenant Parks stood up, fighting the temptation to yawn. He wasn't bored or indifferent; he was just very tired.

"There were no signs around the house of a struggle or anything?"

Sherwood's head jerked up and stared at the other man.

"Why no. But what do you think . . . "

"I don't think anything—yet," the lieutenant said. "Anyway, you've made a formal report downstairs, is that right?"

"That's right. But . . . "

"Okay, I'm going to have a man go out and look your place over. We can handle the routine end from here. You've given us the license number and make of the car, a description and so forth?"

"Yes."

"All right, I'll have one of our men run out home with you. He may turn up something. And in the meantime, try not to worry. We'll find her, all right. Probably nothing at all. Maybe she just . . . . "

Sherwood turned away, a defeated, baffled expression in his eyes.

"I'd go out with you myself," the lieutenant said, "but we're pretty busy here just now. As you may have heard, an armored car was stuck up in town this morning and the thugs got away with close to a quarter of a million dollars. A guard was shot. He died up in County Hospital about an hour ago."

He pushed a button on his desk and a moment later the door opened and Coogins put his head in.

"Get Detective Sims," Parks said.

As they waited for the detective to arrive, the lieutenant took a cigarette from a crumpled pack and then offered the pack to Sherwood, who shook his head.

"By the way, do you know if your wife was carrying any particularly large amount of money with her? Or wearing any valuable jewelry or anything?"

For a moment, Sherwood almost smiled.

"Junk jewelry, if she was wearing anything. I doubt even that. Joyce doesn't care for jewelry. As far as money goes, she probably didn't have more than four or five dollars in her bag. She never carries anything much. When she shops she usually pays with a check. Makes it easier for her to keep track of things."

"And nothing was missing from the house? Nothing of value?"

"Nothing." For a second Sherwood looked thoughtful and then quickly he looked up. "Flick," he said.

"What?"

"Flick—our poodle. He's gone too. He was with Joyce in the car this morning when she took me to the station. And now he's gone too. I don't know why it didn't occur to me before."

"That's odd," Lieutenant Parks said, rather aimlessly. It occurred to him that maybe this wasn't just a routine case after all. It was true that plenty of young women left their husbands for one reason or another. But they usually didn't bother to do so without packing a few clothes. And they didn't usually take off with a poodle.

The door opened and a heavy-shouldered, middle-aged

man wearing a gray fedora slanted over one eye entered the room.

"Want you to meet Mr. Sherwood," Lieutenant Parks said. "Mr. Sherwood's wife is missing."

2.

CRIBBINS had taken no chances about the car. When Mitty left the rooming house at six o'clock that Monday morning he walked to the door with him, gave him a pat on the back as the thick-set, short-armed man squeezed through the opening and started down the steps.

"Just don't rush it," he said. "There's plenty of time. But keep an eye on your watch and be sure to be back here no later than eight-fifteen."

Mitty was gone now and Cribbins had returned to the large room they shared and poured himself a second cup of coffee from the electric percolater which he kept in violation of the local health ordinance.

Yes, he'd been smart about the car and he wasn't trusting to luck. Not that there was anything tricky about picking up a hot car—anyone could have figured that part out. But he'd gone a step further.

Just any old car wouldn't do, even with the switched plates. It had to be a very particular type of car. An unobtrusive car, but a new, fast job. And it had to be safe. Safe for at least the few short hours they would be needing it. He wouldn't take any chance on their being picked up before they had completed the operation. That's why he'd cased the doctor's house for weeks on end, making sure that the doctor returned from the hospital around three o'clock in the morning, every Monday, week in and week out. That once home, he left the car on the street in front of his house and went in and went to bed and didn't get up until afternoon. That no one got up and no one used the car.

Taking it, of course, would be routine—just a simple matter of switching the wires, and at that Mitty was adept. Once away from the apartment house, the business of changing the plates for the phony ones—for which he had the forged license papers—would take only a minute. And then they'd be perfectly safe.

It was just one extra little precaution, but it was typical of the way he planned the job. All those extra little precautions. They were the difference which would make a highly speculative venture turn into a highly successful one. It was all a simple matter of detail and timing.

Cribbins looked down at the stainless steel watch on his wrist, knowing without thinking about it that it would show the correct time. Harry Cribbins was an extremely meticulous and precise man. Well, for this sort of thing you had to be precise. Split-second timing was absolutely essential. Every little piece had to fall into place at exactly the right moment. For a quarter of a million dollars you could afford to be precise. In fact, if you wanted to stay out of prison, and possibly out of the electric chair, you couldn't afford to be anything else. It was what he'd been incessantly drilling into those others who were in on the thing with him, from the very beginning when he'd first begun planning the job.

It had taken some drilling too. God knows he didn't have much to work with. But beggars—or thieves, to be more exact—couldn't be choosers.

Cribbins smiled wryly, but his pale gray eyes remained cold and calculative.

Take Mitty. Mitty certainly wasn't much and he doubted if any other mob in the country would have trusted that rather dim-witted, punchy man whose face bore the scars of a hundred lost battles. But Mitty was loyal and would do exactly as he was told to do. He didn't ask questions and there was no doubt but what the ex-pug's amazing physical strength would be of value, if properly used. The trick with Mitty was to give him no problem which would strain the delicate balance of his mentality.

Harry Cribbins remembered back to the time he'd first met Karl Mitty. It was Goldman who had brought them together and he recalled his surprise that Goldman would have a dimwit hanging around. He'd asked Goldman about it, later, when the two of them were alone.

"Sure," the lawyer had told him, "he's a little punchy. Some of his marbles are gone, but he has his points. He's big and he's tough, and the few things he knows he knows well. There isn't a better hot-car artist around. The only thing is, he's just too stupid to know what to do with a car when he gets one. He takes 'em for pleasure, for God's sake."

Goldman had met Mitty while the big boy was still able to get a fight in one of the smaller clubs. He began to use him as a sort of errand boy and hanger-on, but after a while when Mitty would get in minor jams, Goldman tried to get rid of him. It was Goldman who'd worked an angle and got Mitty the job as a beer truck driver for Rumplemyer's. Of course the job hadn't lasted very long. None of Mitty's jobs lasted.

"Maybe you can use him," Goldman had told Cribbins. "God knows what for, though," he'd added cryptically. "He's strong as an ox, and fearless. Willing to do anything, just so you tell him what to do."

It was funny how Mitty had taken to Cribbins right from the first. Mitty figured Cribbins was a smart cookie who might put him in line for something. Harry Cribbins had to laugh when he thought about how it had actually turned out. It really was ironic that it worked exactly the other way around; that it was Mitty who'd put him, Harry Cribbins, onto the possibilities of the Rumplemyer job.

Yeah, Mitty was all right. You just had to know how to handle him, what to do with him. Mitty was like a piece of machinery, like the big car that right now he was stealing, or like a sub-machine gun—dangerous, powerful, and with no vestige of intelligence. It was necessary only to make sure he had the proper direction. Like a gun, Mitty was as safe or as dangerous as the person who used him.

Santino was something else again. Santino was always dangerous.

Harry Cribbins lifted the coffee cup to his lips and at the same time his eyes went to the cot against the wall, where the slight figure lay under the shabby blanket. Santino hadn't awakened when he and Mitty had gotten up and put on their clothes.

Santino slept like a dead man, or rather a dead man with St. Vitus dance. He twitched and jerked and his half-open mouth emitted tiny sounds, but he never awakened, never opened his eyes. Nothing bothered him, once he'd had his shots and climbed between the covers. He dreamed and slept on and his dreams must have been wild and violent and filled with strange and terrible things, because he moaned and talked all night long. But he didn't wake up.

His dreams were like his daylight hours, which also were filled with violence and terrible things.

Once more Cribbins's eyes went to the watch and he figured that he could let Santino sleep a while longer. There was time enough then, plenty of time. It would take only a few minutes for him to do what he had to do.

Santino was a junkie and he had a sharp, evil mind and an uncontrollable temper. But he also had maniacal courage and a particular way with guns. A man like Santino was essential for the thing they had planned. Someone had to handle the Tommy gun and it had to be someone who would use it with unerring skill if the necessity arose. Cribbins hoped that the necessity wouldn't arise, but he had to be prepared. There was one thing, however; he'd get rid of the little man the very second they made the split. Where he, Cribbins, would go, once he had his share, none of them would know and none would ever find out.

In a sense it was too bad he couldn't take Luder along with him. Luder was the only one of the whole bunch for whom he had any real affection. They had been friends for a long time, since the days when they had been doing a stretch in the big house together. He liked and trusted Luder. But Luder, like the others, had a flaw in his make-up, and it was a dangerous flaw—controllable temporarily, but dangerous in the long run. Luder was a drunk. True, only a periodic drunk, but a drunk nevertheless.

He knew that he could trust Luder to stay sober while they were pulling the job. He knew the old man wouldn't dream of taking a drink then. But later on, when everything was over and done with, and when they had the money and everything would seem safe, that's when he'd crack. That's when he'd let down the bars and take a drink. And one drink would lead to another and another and then another, and Luder would no longer be safe.

No, much as he liked Luder, he'd have to desert him, along with the others, once the thing was over and done with. Thinking about it, his mind went from Luder to the girl. To Paula. Paula, probably asleep this very moment in the house up in the little town at the other end of the county. Paula, who was holding down the place they'd picked for the temporary hideout while the heat cooled off. Paula, who was supposed to be Santino's girl and who had been shacking up with the little gunman when Cribbins had first found him.

For several moments then, as he lighted a fresh cigarette and drew long draughts on it, he thought of Paula and of Santino. He still couldn't understand it. They had been living together, but Cribbins knew Santino merely paid the girl's rent and kept a room himself in a cheap downtown hotel. Paula was supposed to have been on the habit but had kicked it, and Cribbins couldn't for the world see what kept them seeing each other. He knew she hated and feared the little junkie. And Santino himself paid almost no attention to her, with the exception of an occasional curse when he didn't like the food she cooked for him or when she was slow in handing him something he wanted.

There was no doubt about it, Paula held a certain fascination for him. She's like an animal, he thought. Like a beautiful, well-groomed animal. She'd come to him if he wanted her. All she needed was someone who would be kind to her and would give her love. For a long time, when he'd first met her, he'd wondered what went on behind those great dark eyes of hers, what odd and strange thoughts were concealed by the low, smooth forehead under the blue-black hair. But after a while he learned that there were no thoughts, there was nothing at all. Paula merely lived and breathed and felt.

She was in her early twenties, a slender, rather small girl with a beautiful, rounded figure, thin-waisted and trim, but with a ripe and fully matured body. She was a woman who had been made for one purpose, and on Santino that purpose was utterly wasted.

Cribbins knew that he'd picked her up some place out in Pennsylvania, where she'd been working as a waitress. He'd brought her to New York and put her on the junk. She was good-looking and young and Santino had no difficulty in getting her work in a nightclub. He probably had other plans, too, but whatever they were, nothing had happened. Even Santino had realized that Paula wasn't to be trusted. She'd talk, sooner or later; she was bound to. Not because she would rebel or fight what he wanted her to do; it was just that she was simple and that some time or other she'd run into someone who would be kind to her and then she'd start talking.

Cribbins himself had been kind to her and she'd reacted as he knew she would. But Cribbins had been very careful. He could have taken her, but he didn't because he didn't want to lose Santino. He needed Santino; he couldn't risk any trouble, not before they did what they had to do.

For a fleeting moment, Cribbins entertained the idea of taking Paula along when the gang split. But almost at once he discarded it. Paula was known to be Santino's girl and there was every chance that sooner or later Santino would be picked up. Cribbins couldn't take a chance on being saddled with anyone who might tie him in with Santino once he was free and clear.

For a moment he thought of reaching for the telephone and giving her a ring, just to see if everything was all right at the other end. But then he quickly discarded the idea. Everything would be all right; there was no point in taking any chances. A telephone call could always be traced.

Once more he looked down at his watch. It was time Luder was getting in touch. Almost simultaneously the telephone rang and he quickly reached for the receiver. Luder was calling exactly on the dot.

"I've got the van, and I'm about to leave."

Cribbins merely said "Good," and then hung up. He walked across the room to the cot on which Santino slept.

Charlie Luder considered himself a family man. It was a rather odd conceit in view of the fact that Luder hadn't seen his wife or his three children in more than twenty years. Most of those years had been spent behind bars and when they'd finally let him out, Luder knew too much time had passed and that the boys were now grown up and his wife was an old woman. He made it a point not to look them up, not to let them know his address.

But he was a man who'd always hated to be alone and so he had taken a small apartment in the upper Bronx and set up bachelor quarters. He was an old man now and it never occurred to him to seek a new woman. Instead, he adopted a cat from a neighboring butcher and then a week or so later, bought a dog of dubious ancestry from a pet shop. He worked for a while at odd jobs, making very little money and needing very little. And then Cribbins had looked him up and he'd decided to go in with him on the plan.

That weekend he'd taken care of the things he had to take care of. First there was the truck. He bought it legitimately from a second-hand dealer, using an assumed name and giving a false address. It wasn't much of a truck, being actually a beaten-up old moving van of ancient vintage, but it would serve the purpose.

He didn't mind giving up the apartment and he didn't bother to remove the few sticks of furniture. His personal possessions could be packed into a briefcase. It was harder saying good-by to the dog and the cat, for he was inordinately fond of both of them. That was one thing about Luder—he loved animals. Even when he went on his periodical benders he'd always remember to feed and water them.

And so on that last Saturday when he got all through checking the place for any possible thing which left behind might point to him, he'd taken the two animals down to the Bide-A-Wee home and left them.

He left the apartment for the last time shortly after seven on Monday morning and walked over to the parking lot where he'd left the moving truck. He wore a windbreaker and a peaked cap, and although it was a warm day his hands were protected by leather gloves.

The truck was slow to start for a moment or so, as the motor slowly turned over, he had a quick sense of alarm. But then at last it caught and he wheeled the old five-ton van out into the street and headed for Route 1.

He stopped at a diner in Rye and put in his phone call. Then he went back to the counter and ordered a large breakfast. He had plenty of time. Brookside was not more than a few miles up the line and he didn't want to get there too early. He was thinking how much he'd hated to part with the dog as he sipped his coffee and waited for the little dark-eyed waitress to bring the ham and scrambled eggs.

While Luder was waiting for his breakfast in the roadside diner in Rye, Santino slowly came out of his deep sleep. He pulled himself off the bed, his thin, pinched face hollow-eyed and deeply lined and he stretched his wasted arms and yawned. Wordlessly he stared for a moment or two at Cribbins, then stood up and went to the sink in the corner of the room. He washed sketchily and dried his face and hands on a soiled turkish towel.

Santino had only removed his shoes and loosened his tie when he'd turned in so it took him very little time to get ready. He waited until after he'd put on the faded jacket and pulled the cap over his eyes before he went to the closet and took out the worn cardboard suitcase.

Cribbins watched him without speaking, as he snapped open the latches on the suitcase and inspected its contents. He seemed satisfied, and reclosed the bag. He checked his watch, which he carried in his trouser pocket.

Cribbins suggested a cup of coffee, but Santino shook his head.

"I'll get one outside," he said. He was leaving as Mitty returned. The two nodded briefly, passing each other in the doorway.

Carefully closing and locking the door, Mitty turned to face Cribbins and shrugged his thick shoulders.

"A real sour ball, that one," he said.

Cribbins nodded. "Yeah, but he knows his job, and that's what counts. How about the car?"

"Out front," Mitty said. "All set."

Cribbins got up and moved over to the dresser. He pulled open the second drawer from the top and reaching in, lifted out the uniform.

"Okay, let's get started then."

He tossed the clothes over to Mitty and then opened the top drawer and took out another collection of garments. "We'll get dressed," he said, "and then start cleaning up this place. When we leave it will be for the last time and I want to be sure there are no prints or anything—just in case."

He had to remove the shoulder holster which held the .38 Police Special which he was never without, in order to get into the blue flannel shirt.

Santino felt like hell. He coughed, a hollow, wracking cough, as he walked down the steps from the rooming house and into the bright sunlight of the fresh morning. It was a beautiful day, already warm, and promising hot, dry heat for later in the afternoon. The charm of the early fresh morning air was, however, lost on the little man.

He never felt good in the mornings. It wasn't until later, some time around noon after he'd had his first needle, that he really began to feel good. Feeling good, for Santino, wasn't like feeling good for most men. With

Santino it was largely negative; a sense of suspension when his mind would wander and he'd live in a sort of half-world of fantasy and dreams.

He rounded the corner and as he walked, with quick, jerky steps, he pulled a package of cigarettes from his coat pocket and tore open the top of the package. In spite of the cough he lighted one and drew deep puffs. He choked then for a moment and cleared his throat and spit.

He went directly to the small restaurant a couple of blocks away and stopped outside long enough to buy a morning tabloid. Entering, he found a stool at the counter and ordered black coffee. That waitress asked if he wanted anything else and he growled a quick "no." He read the paper as he drank the coffee, turning at once to the back pages and checking the race track results.

When he finished with the charts, he went back and started with the front section. He read only the headlines and the captions under the pictures. His eyes lingered longest over the scattered photographs of seminude girls—chorus girls whose pictures were used largely for decorative purposes and other girls who had made the publicity grade because of lawsuits or current jams with the police. His eyes were shadowed and lecherous as he slowly absorbed the pictures; in his mind he was committing all sorts of unspeakable acts.

Twenty minutes after he'd entered the restaurant, he paid his check and left. He had to walk another several blocks before he came to the cab stand.

The driver left him in the middle of the block, several hundred yards from the place where'd he'd rented the garage. He walked the rest of the way and when he reached the garage, he took a key from his pocket and opened the heavy padlock. The pushcart was where he had left it several nights before. There was no light in the garage but he didn't need one. His thin, nervous hands darted under the canvas tarpaulin which covered the cart and he found what he knew would be there. He grunted with satisfaction.

Five minutes later he left, pushing the cart in front of him. It was only a matter of a few blocks to the intersection. He didn't have to check his watch; he knew that he was going to be there on time.

For the first time he smiled; he had a strange sense of

exhilaration and pleasure. He was looking forward to what was going to happen, what he had to do. It was just as it always was—the kick he got out of it in advance and in contemplation. He felt like a man going to keep a date with a new and promising woman. He was hoping that everything would go smoothly, but at the same time he was secretly wishing in the back of his mind that there might be just the slightest hitch; that there might be an excuse to reach under that canvas which covered the cart.

A thin, puny, weak man, Santino had a fatal fascination for violence. Violence made a giant out of him.

3.

No one is hurt. That was the first thought which crossed her mind as she stepped to the pavement from the car. Yes, thank God, no one seemed to be hurt; both men had gotten out to inspect the damage and they seemed to be all right. She herself was shaken up and Flick, the poodle, was howling blue murder but both of them were all right. Even the cars didn't seem too badly damaged.

Joyce Sherwood gave a pathetic little laugh as her eyes took in the uniforms of the two policemen. Just her luck—running into a couple of cops. And it was her fault, no doubt of that. Well, at least she was insured, which was a help. She moved toward the front of the car where the two men stood silently as they checked to see how bad it was.

They'll probably give me a ticket, she thought. And the dealer will knock a few dollars off of what he was going to give me on the turn-in allowance. But it could have been a lot worse—a whole lot worse . . . .

Cribbins swore softly under his breath.

"Damn—damn it to hell," he said. "It couldn't be worse. That fool woman . . ."

Mitty looked down at the puddle of water forming under the crumpled grillework of the almost new, two-toned Caddie. "Got the radiator, all right," he said.

Cribbins's eye went at once to his watch and his mind

went simultaneously to a certain spot several miles away where he knew a pushcart would be sitting against a curb and where a broken-down old moving van would be waiting around the corner, waiting to pull across the road at exactly nine thirty-two. Went to the spot where the armored car would be passing in another twelve minutes and thirty seconds.

It would take a lot more than twelve minutes and thirty seconds before the Caddie moved again, at least under its own power.

Joyce stood next to Cribbins and looked at the damage and slowly shook her head. "I'm so sorry," she said. "It was all my fault. I just didn't quite see you in time and my mind was on . . ."

Both men turned and stared at her.

For a moment she hesitated. There was something very strange about the way they were looking at her and instinctively her hand tightened its grip on the bag she held. This would spoil everything. Her mind went at once to the surprise which she had planned for Bart's birthday.

The way the two of them were looking at her, she began to suspect that it wasn't just going to be a simple matter of an apology and maybe a ticket. Why, they might even arrest her and take her to jail. She could imagine Bart coming home from the office in time to bail her out! It would make a swell birthday present. Just great. Instead of the brand-new convertible sitting in the driveway to greet him, there would be a message to come down to the jailhouse and get his wife. She felt like crying.

"I'm—I'm afraid a piece of my bumper seems to have punctured your radiator," Joyce said hesitantly.

The two men continued to stare at her. For a moment she wondered why they didn't say anything—why they didn't ask for her license. It was the first thing that policeman always did—ask to see your license.

She began to fumble with her leather bag and then again she suddenly remembered the cashier's check for twenty-six hundred dollars, neatly folded up in the celluloid case which held her driving license. She remembered what the teller had said to her as he handed her the check.

"Made out like that, to cash, it's just like money. So be careful of it," he'd warned her. Joyce had never carried more than a hundred dollars in cash at one time with her in her whole life.

Her eyes went again to the wreckage of the two cars and for the first time it occurred to her that the Caddie was not an official police car. It must belong to one of the officers. No wonder the man seemed shocked.

"I *am* insured," Joyce said in a weak voice.

Cribbins turned abruptly to Mitty. "Get in and see if you can back it off," he ordered.

As Mitty climbed into the driver's seat, he looked at Joyce.

"Start your motor, lady," he said. "See if your heap is okay."

The moment the two cars separated he saw what had happened. It was one of those freak things that wouldn't take place one time in a hundred. The bracket holding the license plate on the old sedan had twisted at the moment of impact and had pierced through the grillwork of the other car and slashed into the radiator. With the exception of this, neither automobile was more than scratched.

Joyce still sat behind the wheel of her car as Mitty stepped to the street again and the two men spoke together for a moment. They turned and started toward her.

Flick barked and Joyce quickly shushed him. It was then she noticed for the first time that both men were wearing gloves. Gloves, in June! She noticed it because she was watching Cribbins and as he approached, he lifted his left hand and pushed back his blue serge sleeve to once more look at his watch.

At this particular point a lesser man than Cribbins would undoubtedly have given up and called the whole thing off. This completely pointless and unexpected accident was the one possible event which he had been unable to foresee and unable to prepare for. It threw his entire timetable out of kilter; caught him at a point where it was impossible to postpone or revise his master plan and at the same time created a situation making it difficult if not totally impossible to proceed. Not only had the accident ruined his means of getting away once the job was accomplished; it was now unlikely they would arrive at the scene of the impending drama in time to participate.

And there was no way of letting Santino and Luder know. They would be there, ready to go into action the moment the armored car arrived on the scene. And where would he and Mitty be? They'd be several miles away discussing a petty traffic accident with a girl and her dog.

That one look at his watch told Cribbins everything. There was no time now to find another car; no time to do anything but head directly to the spot where he had his rendezvous. The only car available was this other one; the car belonging to the girl who had run into them. They could take the car all right, although it wasn't much of a car at best, but what about the girl? Certainly they couldn't leave her to spread the alarm. There was only one thing to do—take her with them and hope for the best. He would have to play it by ear from here on in.

Cribbins spoke to Mitty, who quickly went back to the Caddie. He himself moved to the side of the old sedan. Without a word he opened the back door and climbed in. He took the revolver from its holster as Joyce craned her neck to turn and look at him with wide, alarmed eyes.

"Move over in the seat," he said. "And keep your mouth shut. Do just as I tell you and maybe you won't get hurt. And shut that damned dog up."

For a moment then she was too startled to do anything but sit and stare at him. She was too startled to be frightened.

"I said move over!"

Joyce slowly closed her mouth and then, without consciously thinking about it, slid from under the wheel. Mitty had returned from the Caddie and he tossed a leather bag into the back of the car. He opened the door on the driver's side.

"See here," Joyce suddenly said, her voice inordinately high. "See here! You don't need to point that gun at me. I'm not a criminal, you know."

She fought to avoid the hysteria she felt coming over her.

"You're not," Cribbins said. "But I am. So shut up and do just what I tell you to do." His eyes went to Mitty. "Get started," he ordered. "We can make it if you hurry. But be careful—we don't want to be stopped. Not now."

Mitty rammed the car into gear and Flick began barking wildly.

For a second Mitty hesitated and then he spoke over his shoulder. "Shouldn't we at least get rid of the mutt?" he asked.

Cribbins shook his head. "No," he said. "The dog is likely to come in handy. Very handy."

Wordlessly, Mitty swung the car around and headed for

the Post Road. After a moment or two, he slowly shook his head and muttered under his breath.

"My Gawd," he said. "I never thought I'd start out on a caper with a girl and a French poodle!"

Old Paul Rumplemyer had a reputation for being a character. Among the many people who knew him, some said that he was a typically smart Dutchman, others called him an eccentric, and a few considered him nothing more or less than a throwback to a dying age. Almost no one disliked him and a great many, especially tavern keepers whom he had helped through the lean years, considered him a philanthropist.

Paul's father, Otto Rumplemyer, had emigrated to America from Bavaria around the turn of the century and within a year or two of arriving had started Rumplemyer's Brewery. He wasn't an overambitious man and had been satisfied to run a small, tightly knit operation, being content to brew the very best beer he knew how to brew and confine his business to a select number of German and Irish saloons.

Paul grew up in the business and along about the time the old man was ready to retire and go back to Germany, shortly before World War I, Paul took over.

He was in his twenties at the time, but knew all he needed to know to run the business successfully. Being of German descent, he found the war a little difficult, but he managed to keep the business going. When prohibition came along, he continued to do business, as usual. He changed to near-beer, of course, but he found means of supplying his buyers with the necessary ingredients to spike his product, and thus continued to prosper.

His was one of the few firms which did continue to brew beer and at the same time avoid being taken over by the new crop of gangsters who had been sired by the dry vote.

Prohibition ended and another war came and went, but Paul Rumplemyer went on much as usual. The city had grown vastly and Rumplemyer's Brewery grew right along with it. But it remained essentially a local operation. The only change Paul made was to move the plant into Westchester, north of the city, where land and taxes were cheaper.

Times and methods changed with the years, but neither Paul Rumplemyer nor his brewery changed with them.

He continued to brew the same high-quality product in the same way his father had brewed it before him. He continued to handle his employees in the same paternalistic fashion and conduct his business along the lines which had been satisfactory for more than half a century.

Rumplemyer's drivers, even in the old days when deliveries were made in great beer wagons drawn by four-in-hand teams of lumbering Percherons, had always made their own sales and deliveries and collections. They'd leave each morning loaded down with kegs, and when they'd return in the evening their first stop was in the main office where they'd turn over the day's receipts to the cashier. More often than not, Paul himself would be standing by to check the figures. At night the money was locked up in an ancient safe. With the passing of years and the advent of fast, efficient trucks, the uneconomical and impractical wagons were discarded and a fleet of motor vans took their place. But the ancient practices continued.

On the first Monday of each month an armored car would arrive at the gates of the brewery and be admitted. The money would then be transferred to the local branch of a Manhattan bank. Bank officials, friends and even his insurance company had often discussed this situation with Paul Rumplemyer and had warned the old man that keeping so large an amount of money in the old office safe was dangerous business. They said it was an open invitation to anyone who wanted to stick up the place.

But the old man would merely laugh and shrug his shoulders. Hell, he had a night watchman, didn't he? A man who never left the office which held the safe and stayed there with a double-barreled shotgun across his lap. Another thing, there never had been any trouble, never any attempt made to break into the place. The system had always worked satisfactorily and he wasn't going to change. Somehow or other he liked the idea of that money piling up there, day after day, for a whole month. When he did make a deposit, it was a respectable one.

Old Paul wasn't going to change his habits for anyone. He'd gone through prohibition, when the toughest mobsters of all time had been around, trying to move in on him. They hadn't, though, and he certainly wasn't going to start worrying about stickups this late in the game. As a matter of fact, he was partly right. The Rumplemyer

Brewery would have been a very tough nut for anyone to crack. That safe was a lot stouter than it looked. It would take dynamite to blast it and the way the plant was located, right in the heart of the industrial section, no one would ever have a chance to blow it up and still find time to make a getaway before the cops were on them.

There was only one trouble with the old man's system. It gave ulcers to the driver of the armored car who had to make the monthly pickups. Not only did he have to start work an hour earlier than usual in order to be at the brewery in time to get loaded and away by nine o'clock—which Rumplemyer insisted upon—but he knew that he was carrying somewhere around a quarter of a million dollars and this upset him.

The armored car system which Rumplemyer's used was a small local outfit and they specialized in payrolls, which never amounted to more than twenty or thirty thousand. They weren't really equipped for big jobs, and the drivers were aware of just how vulnerable they were. After all, those half-ton trucks which they drove were called armored cars more by courtesy than anything else. They were slow, cumbersome vehicles, usually a dozen or more years old, and carried neither modern equipment nor burglarproof armor.

There was only the driver, who wore a revolver at his side, and a second man who sat back in the truck part of the vehicle. He too wore a gun and he also had a shotgun strapped to hooks next to him. A solid blow with a hammer would be sufficient to break the lock on the double back doors of the truck.

Red Kenny, who'd been driving the car which had been making the money pickups from the brewery for the last couple of years, knew that the ancient hack he drove could be outdistanced by a boy on a fast English bike. He, for one, figured Paul Rumplemyer was not only eccentric; he thought he was downright crazy. One other thing frequently bothered Red. He was a big beer drinker and particularly liked Rumplemyer's beer. It made him furious to arrive there and hang around while the money was placed in the truck and not even be offered as much as a single cool glass of the beverage. He was thinking just that as, thirty-one minutes after nine, he turned into the Old Post Road and started to drive south along the all but deserted street.

The new Post Road was a couple of blocks to the left, paralleling the old road, and almost all of the through traffic used it. Red would have liked to use it himself, but he drove the route which the old man had prescribed years ago and which he would never allow to be changed.

Carl Slagher put his head into the small opening between the rear and the driver's compartment and spoke in a hoarse voice, yelling to make himself heard above the clamor of the truck. "Hurry it up a little, boy," Carl said, "and we can dump this in time to pick up a beer before getting back to the office."

Carl liked his beer too. In fact, it was largely because of this fatal weakness that he'd been let go by the police force a few years back and had to take the job as guard on the truck. The truck company, being a small outfit and not too prosperous, was unable to be choosy about whom it hired. Honesty and a willingness to work for low pay were the only two requisites.

Red half turned to shout an answer to the other man, but as he did, he saw the pushcart standing a little away from the curb several hundred feet down the street. Quickly he turned back and swung out to give it plenty of room.

The pushcart was on the right-hand side of the street, just before an intersection. As Red pulled the truck toward the middle of the road, a big moving van swung in from the intersection at his left. It was moving fast, considering it was turning into a cross street, and it made a wide curve.

For a brief second Red almost shouted, knowing that if the driver didn't cut his turn short, he'd be bound to crash into his own vehicle. Red was going only about twenty-five miles an hour and instinctively he jammed his feet on the brake pedal and the clutch, cutting back a little, but not too much, as he didn't want to smash into the pushcart.

A second later he did yell, but by then it was too late. The driver of the moving van failed to straighten his lumbering machine and it smashed into the side of the armored car.

For a moment it seemed the vehicle would topple over on its side, and Red's face paled as he tried to cling to the wheel. The armored car teetered for a moment and then straightened as the van pushed it into the curb.

The shock threw Carl Slagher to the hard iron floor in the rear of the vehicle, and he was knocked unconscious. The door opposite Red flew open. He fell across the seat and half out of the car.

Cribbins sat in the back of the sedan and stared at the crystal of his watch. He held the gun in his lap, the muzzle pointed at the girl's head.

It had really been a beautiful plan.

The armored car would reach the intersection at nine thirty-two. And just as it approached, Luder would swing into the road with the heavy van and crash into it. In that split second, while the men in the truck were still dazed, he and Mitty would pull up in the Caddie, dressed in the fake police uniforms. They'd be there just the crucial moment, in time to drag the driver and the guard from the armored car. By the time the men came to, assuming they weren't badly injured—and they shouldn't be, at the speed the truck would be going—he'd have everything in hand.

Mitty would pretend to arrest Luder, while Cribbins herded the two men from the armored car into the Caddie. They'd take the three money bags along, ostensibly to go to the police station and thrash the whole thing out. There would be no reason for the guards to be suspicious. They couldn't expect to leave the money there in the wrecked car.

And then there was Santino, just in case; Santino standing by the pushcart, with the sub-machine gun concealed under the canvas. They'd get him into the Caddie, too, if everything went all right, as a witness to the accident. Once in the car it would be duck soup. They'd disarm the guards and head for the country; for the back roads which he'd mapped out and for the spot where they'd leave the two men tied up and gagged.

By the time the wreckage was found, they'd be well on their way. And by the time the guards were found, they wouldn't have to be worrying about road blocks or anything else at all. They'd be up at the other end of the county, safe in the hide-out.

It was just about as foolproof as it could be: a fast car, no witnesses left around to identify them. It was perfect. Perhaps except for this damned fool girl who had smashed into the Caddie. Now they had no getaway car, or at least nothing but this pile of junk they were riding in. Now it was a question whether they'd even get there in time for the crash.

Cribbins cursed under his breath. A fat lot of good his plans were going to be now. A lot of good the police uniforms were going to be. There had been plenty of trouble getting those uniforms, too.

Cribbins leaned forward. "When we get there," he said, "pull around the corner. Out of sight of the truck. You stay in the car with the girl and keep her quiet. Stay until we get back to you."

Mitty nodded. He wondered what was in the other man's mind. He was beginning to wish that Cribbins would tell him to just keep right on going. Not stop at all. He couldn't see how it could be worked now.

He slowed down and started to swing the car into the Old Post Road, a block from where Luder was to crash the truck into the armored car. As he did the sudden sharp staccato of a sub-machine gun reached his ears.

Cribbins quickly leaned over his shoulder. "Right to it," he said in a tight, hard voice. "Drive right to it." He lifted the gun from his lap. He jabbed a lean finger into Joyce Sherwood's back. "If you want to stay alive," he said, "you sit tight. Hang onto that mutt and sit tight. Mitty, you stay with the car. Have your gun ready."

A moment later the old sedan screeched to a halt at the blocked intersection where the truck and the armored car were piled up.

4.

Even if Red Kenny had lived it is doubtful if he would ever have been able to explain why he acted exactly as he did. A psychologist would probably say that he had been conditioned by his job to be suspicious and on the alert and this may have been true. On the other hand, at the time of the crash, when he realized an accident was unavoidable, Red was thinking of nothing except a glass of cold beer.

The fact that it took place exactly where it did very

likely had something to do with it. The armored car, after leaving the brewery, took a prescribed route on its way south to the city. The brewery itself lay at the northernmost fringe of Brookside. Between this section and the main part of the town lay a large residential area of middleclass homes which were growing old and dilapidated.

When the new throughway was put in a couple of years back, block after block of these homes were condemned and gradually builders came in and bought up the land to build modern garden apartments. The Old Post Road ran through this section and for a number of blocks along its length the land was torn up and awaiting improvement.

The spot where the accident took place was in a particularly deserted stretch and there were no houses or buildings within several square blocks. The land had been partially cleared, but new construction hadn't as yet started. The old road itself was a sorry mess and virtually all traffic avoided it; Red himself would have preferred to.

The moment Red saw the pushcart at the side of the deserted road, something told his subconscious that it didn't belong there. There was no reason for its being there. But before he had a chance to think of this, the moving van swung into the street and crashed into him and the next thing he knew was when he found himself on the floor, half in and half out of the door.

Raising his head, he looked out and he saw the pushcart standing there a few yards away. There was a man at the side of the cart and he had his back to Red. He was reaching under a canvas which covered the brokendown old cart. Red reached for his own gun. It was pure instinct.

At the moment the two vehicles crashed, Santino thought the moving van Luder was driving was going to push the armored car right into him. He leaped aside and rounded the pushcart to get out of the way. Santino was on edge. Even as he moved, he was cursing under his breath. He'd been watching the armored car approach and he had also been looking past it up the road.

Cribbins and Mitty should have been in sight, but they weren't. It never occurred to Santino that anything could have happened to them; he merely assumed that they were careless and were going to be a few seconds late. But a few seconds could make a lot of difference.

It was because he was looking for the Caddie that he

had almost missed seeing the accident and had to jump. He didn't want to be pinned in the wreckage. It looked for a moment as though the van was going to topple the the other car, but at last the two vehicles came to a stop and the truck was still upright. Only the driver wasn't behind the wheel. That's when Santino started to reach for the sub-machine gun. He still had his hands under the canvas when he swung back once more to the wreckage.

The door of the armored car had sprung open and a man was half lying on the floor. There was a gun in the man's hand and he was so close that Santino could see the color of his eyes. They were blue-green, and they looked almost sightless. There was a nasty bruise on the man's forehead and it was bleeding badly.

As Santino watched, frozen for a moment, the man shifted his position and lifted the hand which held the gun to wipe the blood from his forehead. In that second Santino jerked the submachine gun from the pushcart.

Red Kenny was still wiping away the blood, not even seeing Santino at all, when the half-dozen slugs tore open the flesh from his right shoulder to his waist, stitching neat little holes in front and leaving great gaping wounds where they made their exit.

Luder was half out of the truck as Santino loosed the burst of fire and for a moment he stopped, one foot on the pavement and the other still on the running board. He was looking for the Caddie and just realizing it wasn't there where it should be. He stood, half dazed, trying to adjust himself, and then he heard Santino's voice yelling at him.

"There's a car coming! Get the bomb!"

Luder didn't quite understand what was happening but he didn't take time to figure. He followed orders. As he reached the pavement, his hand found the small gas bomb which he carried in the side pocket of his leather jacket. He tossed it through the grille in the back door of the armored car, then turned to see Santino standing next to him with the machine gun raised in his hands.

Cribbins had the back door of the sedan open as Santino raised the gun. He knew at once what was about to happen. Santino was expecting a two-toned Cadillac. Instead he was watching a small black sedan careening to a stop a few yards away.

Cribbins leaped to the street before Mitty had a chance

to brake the car. He yelled as his feet hit the pavement. The yell wasn't quite in time to arrest Santino's finger on the trigger of the gun, but it did serve to spoil his aim. The muzzle swerved as he fired and the burst went into the pavement in front of the sedan.

There was no time to explain; no time for anything but action.

"The crowbar," Cribbins yelled and when Luder just stood there staring at him, he struck the other man a sharp blow on the side of his face and pushed him toward the truck. Luder stumbled and then snapped out of it. Cribbins spoke quickly to Santino as Luder pried open the back door. "Get the money bags into the sedan," he said. "It's our only transportation—no time now to explain. Be careful when you go in the back there. Keep your face covered with a handkerchief."

As Luder and Santino carried the canvas bags out of the truck, Cribbins hurried back to the sedan. He spoke to Mitty, but his eyes were on Joyce Sherwood.

"Get in the back, Mitty," he said. "And get out of that uniform. We've got just about two or three minutes. When Santino and Luder come, explain it to 'em. I'm going to drive and I'll go west as far as the underpass under the parkway, if we don't run into anyone. I want you to get rid of your guns. Put them in the trunk with the money. Have the boys put the money into the trunk."

He hesitated for a moment as he had to raise his arms to jerk the blue uniform shirt over his own head. Under it he wore a white shirt. "Hand me the coat from that suitcase," he ordered.

"We haven't a chance," Mitty said. "They'll git us at the first roadblock."

"Shut up and do as I say," Cribbins snapped. "They won't get you, at least. I'm dumping you and the others at the underpass. You'll just have to try to keep from being picked up. Separate and you'll have a chance. In any case, you'll be clean if they do pick you up. Try and get to the hide-out as soon as you can, but come separately and be damned sure no one tails you."

"How about you? What are you going . . . "

"This little lady is going to drive me up," Cribbins said. "It's our only chance—the only way we can get clear with the money."

"But . . . "

"No buts," Cribbins snapped. "It's the only way. There's just a chance no one will stop a girl and her dog out for a ride in the country with her sick father." He turned then and stared coldly into Joyce's frightened eyes.

A moment later, as Santino and Luder crawled into the back of the sedan, they heard the low wail of a siren off to the south. A block up the street a man was running toward them, waving his arms.

"Stay down in the back," Cribbins said. He released the clutch and as the car moved forward, he spoke to Joyce out of the side of his mouth.

"Get yourself set, sister," he said. "In about ten minutes you're going to take over the wheel. And if you want to stay alive, you'll do exactly what I tell you to do. Just pray that we don't get stopped. You'll be the first one to be shot if we do. And keep the dog on your lap, where it can be seen if we pass anyone. They won't be looking for a dog in a getaway car."

She and Bart had driven over the road a hundred times. Back when they had first started going together—it seemed a century ago but actually she had known Bart for only a year before they were married—they had taken this road to go north for those marvelous ski trips. And then, in the spring, they would come this way on weekends for picnics in the country.

They weren't really picnics, of course, but they would drive until they were some forty or fifty miles north of the city and then turn off the highway and find one of those little towns with an old-fashioned inn and there would be a cocktail or perhaps two cocktails and a long, leisurely lunch and the talk and the plans and everything they were finding together.

Bart had preferred the road to the parkway.

"Sure," he would say, "I know we can make better time on the parkway and I know Twenty-two is always crowded, but the scenery is nice and anyway we aren't in any hurry."

It was absolutely essential that she keep her mind on Bart. The initial shock had worn off; she was past hysteria now, past the point where she might faint, or go into a state of shock. Now it was pure and unadulterated fright.

She must keep her mind busy, think of something, think of anything but that blood-soaked, bullet-ridden armored car driver lying back there beside his truck on the cement pavement. Must think of anything but the lean, hard man who sat tense and waiting at her side.

God, to think that this was she, Joyce Sherwood, celebrating her first wedding anniversary.

She lifted her eyes from the road ahead for a moment and looked at the dogwood trees lining the side of the highway. They had been in bloom on that day of her life when she and Bart had made the one most important drive of all along this road. It was a day which she often remembered and now once more she forced her mind to dwell on it . . . .

They had been going together for quite a while and they'd found a lot to like in each other, but there had been nothing serious. Joyce had been orphaned at an early age and had spent most of her childhood in a convent. Her guardian was a distant relative who lived abroad and had little interest in the child who had been left in his care. He'd shifted his responsibilities to a trust company which in turn had seen to it that Joyce was raised in the convent until she was in her teens. She'd gone to a good finishing school and later had been entered in a New England college.

It was during her sophomore year that the guardian died and shortly after she received the news, the trust company had gotten in touch with her. It seemed that the money for her education had long ago run out and that the distant relative had been paying her expenses out of his own pocket. The first thing his heirs did was to cut off her allowance.

Joyce had to leave the college and take a job. The job was with the Markson Advertising Agency, and it was there that she'd met Bart. Until the time of her first date with him—he took her to dinner after work and then to a movie at one of the midtown art theaters—she'd had almost no contact at all with men. There'd been a couple of dates while she was still in college, but her years in the convent had made her afraid of men and she was extremely shy. Once or twice a boy had tried to kiss her and make love to her but she was embarrassed and frightened and they'd soon given up.

Bart also had tried to kiss her that first night after he had returned with her to the apartment she shared with another girl. Again she had been shy and a little frightened and had pushed him away. Only Bart hadn't given up. He'd been wise and considerate. They continued to see each other outside of the office as well as in it. Gradually she became used to him.

And then came the time they took the drive, planning to spend the day in the country and end up having dinner at the little inn over the line in Connecticut.

Bart was in good spirits and she herself was feeling gay and carefree as they had started out. They'd sung together all the way up, she carrying the tunes of the modern songs and Bart attempting to join her with his deep, soft voice, which never could find the right key. They'd reached the inn early in the afternoon and had gone in and Bart had ordered daiquiries for them. She'd never cared much about drinking, but this day something had happened to her. She was ecstatically happy, for no reason at all except that she was with Bart and it was spring and they were young and full of life.

They had two more drinks apiece and then Bart had ordered the dinner. He'd ordered a very special dinner, sautèed guinea hen and wild rice, and it had taken a while before it would he ready.

While they waited they decided to take a walk and they followed the path behind the inn and down by the little pond. They were standing there at the edge of the pond when Bart had reached over and taken her in his arms and had kissed her. She had acted instinctively then, pushing him and leaning away, and then her feet slipped and the bank began to crumble and the next thing she knew both of them were waist-deep in the pond.

They were laughing wildly as Bart helped pull her out. That's when she suddenly turned to him and raising on her toes, put her arms around him and lifted up her lips.

Ten minutes later they returned to the inn, both dripping wet.

Mama Galuzzi, who ran the place, had thrown up her hands and screamed when she saw them. She yelled at her husband who was cooking in the kitchen and when he came to the door, she spoke to him rapidly in Italian.

Mama Galuzzi took charge. She showed them upstairs and into what must have been her own bedroom. She threw Joyce a great woolly bathrobe and told her to get into it at once. She wouldn't even listen while they tried to argue with her. And then she took Bart down the hall to a second room and handed him a second robe and ordered him to take off his soaking garments. He'd started to protest and she moved in and Bart knew that if he didn't obey she would literally take the clothes off his back. So he, like Joyce, had agreed and had stripped to his skin.

Mama Galuzzi left them up there then while she took their clothes down to the kitchen to dry out.

It was Joyce who walked down and entered the room where Bart sat, hunched up on the edge of the bed. This time there was no hesitation at all when he held out his arms. They didn't even bother to see that the door was locked.

Later on, as they sat opposite each other at the table down in the dining room and ate the guinea hen and wild rice, Mama Galuzzi peeked in on them now and then, a sly smile on her old face.

Bart had tipped her outrageously and they had left, driving back to New York the same way they'd come up, on Route Twenty-two. Neither had talked much on that return trip; neither had to. They knew then that it was all settled. It was just a case of setting the date . . .

Yes, this road would ever be associated in her mind with Bart. It was odd how now, with this sinister, deadly man sitting beside her with his empty right sleeve tucked into the coat of his jacket, she kept thinking of Bart. She didn't want to think of that empty right sleeve. She was too conscious of where the arm was which would normally have filled it. The arm was bent at the elbow and was concealed by his tightly buttoned jacket and his shirt. At the end of that arm was his hand and in the hand was the gun. The gun which was pointed directly at her as she carefully drove the old car.

They had reached Route Twenty-two shortly after dumping the other three, and he had directed her to turn north, through the crowded traffic of the series of suburban towns which were strung out like beads on a necklace. She was surprised, assuming that he'd stick to the back roads.

For a moment or so she'd felt a surge of hope, knowing there would be cars and people. There would undoubtedly be a roadblock, also, sooner or later. They must know about the robbery now, in Brookside. They would have found the armored car with its blood-drenched cargo.

He must have guessed what she was thinking, because he spoke quickly, in that short, clipped voice, which wasn't at all what she thought the voice of a gunman and killer would be, but which pronounced its words clearly and literately, for all of its deadly coldness.

"We may very likely hit a roadblock," he said. "It will be up to you, then. With all this traffic, they'll probably just check your driving license and take a look in the back of the car. If everything is all right, they won't go any further. You pray that they don't. It isn't only that I'll shoot you first; I'll get one of them, anyway, maybe more. I don't have a thing to lose. Remember that—I have nothing to lose. So it isn't just your life you'll be sacrificing. I'll have time to take at least another one along with me. Remember what I have told you. Tell them your right name, show them your license. I'm your father and I've been sick and you're taking me for a ride in the country."

"I'll do what you say," she said.

"You'd better."

They were past Bedford now and still heading north. She remembered the time early in the spring when Bart and she had stopped in Bedford and talked with the real estate agent who had shown them the houses, which were all too expensive. She remembered so many things and suddenly as she thought of Bart she realized that just about now he would be trying to arrange for the theater tickets.

She thought of the check for twenty-six hundred dollars which she had in her purse and of the surprise she had planned for him, the impractical new car which he wanted so badly. She fought to keep the tears back.

A mile or so further on Cribbins told her to slow down and he had her pull off the highway in front of a roadside stand. The carhop came out and smiled at them and Cribbins ordered four hamburgers and a couple of bottles of soda.

"You got change?" he asked, when the girl left to fill the order.

Joyce nodded.

He told the carhop they'd take the food and drinks with them and she didn't realize what he was up to until he made her stop the car a mile further along the road. Then he took the meat from one of the sandwiches and held it out to the dog, who until then had sat stiff and tense between them, growling now and then.

Flick looked at the rare meat and drew back and the man spoke gently. The dog's curly head shot forward and he took a piece of meat. He ate the second sandwich without being coaxed.

"I want him friendly if we get stopped," he said to Joyce.

He told her that she could have the other sandwiches but she shook her head. She wasn't hungry. She did drink one of the bottles of soda.

"What are you going to do with me?" she asked. "Can't you just take the car and let me out and . . . "

He smiled thinly. "You're staying with me," he said. "If I let you out now I'd have to kill you."

She gasped and the wheel jerked in her hands.

"Take it easy," he said. "Nothing's happened to you yet. Maybe nothing will. I don't know myself. Just keep driving."

They went on, passing through Bedford Hills and Golden's Bridge and into the three-laned highway leading to Brewster. It was a mile or two before the Brewster city line that the traffic suddenly became heavy and they were forced to slow down to around twenty-five miles an hour. He was very alert and noticed at once that traffic coming south was normal.

"This is probably it," he said. "Just remember what I told you."

He was right. Within a few hundred yards she had to put the car into second gear and then, as they barely crawled along, they passed a state trooper standing next to his motorcycle at the side of the road. He stared at them as they crawled past him and a moment or so later she had to stop. She could see the line of cars stretching out up ahead.

It took them almost half an hour to reach the point in the highway where the police car was pulled diagonally across the road, blocking the northbound lane.

The car directly in front of them was a low-slung, sporty convertible with its top down. A lone man was behind the wheel. She watched, held in dumb fascination as she saw the two troopers converge. Off to one side, in a second police car, another pair of officers sat. The doors of the police car were open and she could see that the trooper on the outside kept his hand on his holster.

Two state policemen approached the convertible from

each side and the one opposite the driver just stood and leaned against the car and said nothing. The other trooper was asking to see the man's license. While he was getting it out, one of the men from the police car at the side of the road got out and strolled over. He looked into the tonneau of the convertible and then slowly circled until he came to the rear of it. He lifted up the trunk cover and looked inside.

Joyce Sherwood shuddered.

She was thinking of the trunk of her own car; thinking of what lay in it. Not only of the money bags from the wrecked armored car, but the sub-machine gun and the pistols.

Once more Cribbins seemed to sense what was going through her mind. "I'm warning you," he said in a harsh whisper. "Do it just the way I told you to. Don't forget."

Flick growled low in his throat and tensed. A moment later he barked sharp and clear, his feet on the top of the door and his head out the opened window. Cribbins held the dog by his collar and spoke softly to him as the dog continued to bark.

Joyce started to speak, but her companion quickly interrupted. "Let him bark," he said. "Just be sure about yourself."

The driver in the convertible was putting his license back in his wallet. A moment later and they waved him on and signaled for Joyce to move forward. She felt the cruel hard end of the gun poke into her ribs as she slowly released the clutch.

"Smile, damn you," Cribbins whispered. "Smile. Talk with me."

She fumbled with the hand brake as she stopped the car. She knew the color had left her face and she could see her hand trembling on the wheel.

The trooper was at the side of the car now and he was looking at the dog and half grinning. The other one, the one on Cribbins's side, had approached, but he was keeping his distance. He didn't see anything funny at all about the dog.

"Quiet, boy," Cribbins said.

"Like to see your license, miss," the trooper said. "Where are you headed for and where have you come from?"

She spoke as she reached into the leather bag for the license.

"What is it, Officer? What's happened?"

"Just a checkup, miss," he said. He extended his hand and waited.

"We're from Brookside," Joyce said, and the second the words left her mouth she caught the quick sharp look on the trooper's face. At the same time she again felt the prod of the gun in her side.

"I told you you were going a little fast, dear." Cribbins spoke suddenly. He looked at the trooper and frowned in irritation. "My daughter's supposed to be taking me for an airing in the country, but you'd think she was going to a fire." He smiled, and then coughed.

"We're not checking on speeding," the trooper said shortly. He looked down at the license. "Let's have the car registration, too."

He waited until she handed it to him and then looked at it very carefully.

"You're Mrs. Joyce Sherwood?"

"Yes." It came almost in a whisper. She tried to smile again, but couldn't quite make it. "My father's been sick," she said. "I'm taking him for a ride."

"What time did you start out?"

Joyce opened her mouth to speak, but Cribbins quickly cut in. His voice sounded old and querulous.

"Around eight-thirty," he said. "You see we hoped to get up to Pawling in time for lunch and I don't like Joyce to drive too fast."

Joyce felt the car shake slightly and a moment later, as she sat watching the trooper carefully checking her license again, periodically looking up at her to see that the description on the driver's certificate fitted, the trooper who'd been at the rear of the car circled to the side.

"Your trunk's locked, lady," he said. "Mind letting me have the key?"

For a moment she almost forgot her lines in her sudden terror. But the quick pain as Cribbins again poked the gun into her side brought her to. "It isn't locked," she said. "It's jammed. The key was lost and the trunk's jammed and we haven't been able to get it opened."

"I warned you," Cribbins said. "I warned you, Joyce. Said that we might want to be getting into it. What would happen if we should have a puncture or something."

He turned to the trooper and spoke in a tired voice.

"Break it open," he said. "Don't mind if you do. It

would serve her right for not stopping and having it fixed."

The man checking the license looked up at Joyce and smiled. "Guess that won't be necessary," he said. "But you better stop at a garage and get the thing looked at. You might have a flat at that." He handed back the license. "Some dog you got there," he said. He stepped back and waved them on.

As the car pulled away, he turned to the officer who'd failed to get into the trunk. "They were from Brookside," he said.

"Jesus, maybe we should have taken a look in the back," the second trooper said. He seemed nervous.

"Don't be a damned fool," the first one said. "There's a hundred cars passed through here from Brookside and White Plains and down around there. You think that old guy and his daughter pulled the job? Maybe the pooch was the lookout." He laughed and waved the next car toward him. "Anyway," he said, "you heard the old buzzard invite you to break it open, didn't you? Well."

5.

TEN MILES north of Brewster, Cribbins told Joyce to turn off to the left of the road at a macadam intersection. Joyce, following directions, drove on for a few miles and then made a second turn. A mile beyond they entered the town of Cameron Corners.

Cameron Corners is an old farming town. Three or four times in the past fifty years small manufacturing enterprises were started up by local promoters, but little ever came of them. It wasn't until after World War II that the town began to grow at all, largely as a result of an influx of city people looking for weekend places in the country.

The larger of the two grocery stores took additional space and called itself a supermarket, and the other one went out of business. A couple of new gas stations and a second hardware store were opened. Outside of that, and a new open-air theater on the edge of town, very little has changed over the years. The post office was moved from the drugstore into a little one-story building of its own on the main street and that's about it.

Most of the houses had been built in the last part of the nineteenth century and they are painted uniformly white and kept in excellent repair. Lawns are kept trimmed and Cameron Corners remains a typical neat little New England village.

They entered the town from the south and Joyce followed Cribbins's directions, driving down the main street and out to the north end. They passed a number of small houses and he told her to make a left turn. She continued on for two more long blocks and once again he directed her to turn left.

It was a neighborhood of old, Victorian mansions set well back in spacious lawns, shaded by great oaks.

"Second place on the right," he said. "Turn in at the drive and go right on back to the garage."

There was a circular drive, passing the main door in the front and turning then to follow the side of the house. An old-fashioned carriage porch covered the drive.

The house itself was much like its neighbors. Four stories high, surrounded by wide verandas, it was covered with ivy. In its day it had been a fine mansion and the years had failed to alter its impressive dignity.

Behind the main building was the old carriage house, which had been coverted into a garage. Its wide doors stood open and Cribbins directed Joyce to drive inside.

Joyce caught a quick glance of a face at the window as they passed the house. The face of a young, rather pretty girl, her dark eyes wide and startled.

She drove into the garage and just sat behind the wheel until Cribbins's voice brought her back to reality.

"We're here," he said. "Get out. And hang on to that damned dog."

As Joyce stepped to the floor of the carriage house, she noticed the sedan parked next to her own car.

Cribbins had her wait outside the barn and hold the dog by its leash while he pulled the doors closed. It was difficult, using only one hand.

They walked back down the long drive toward the side entrance of the house.

The street out in front was completely deserted and the hot sun-drenched air of midday seemed to hang heavy around them. Joyce shivered involuntarily as they approached the stoop leading up to the porch which circled the house.

Santino watched the car until it turned and swung into the bypass leading up to the overhead road. When it had passed beyond his sight, he slowly dropped his eyes and for a moment just stood there. Then he looked up at the other two men. "The dirty son of a bitch," he said. "This is just great. Here we are, and there he goes with the only car and with the dough."

Mitty didn't say anything, but Luder spoke up. "It's best," he said. "The only thing he could do. This way there's a chance he may make it. The only chance. The four of us would be bound to be stopped. This way there's a chance."

"Yeah—a chance for him," Santino sneered. "But how about us? What happens to us now?"

"We do like he said," Luder said. "Split up. Get back to town and then tomorrow or the next day make it up to the hide-out."

"And I suppose he's just going to stay there waiting with the money, eh?"

Mitty's dull eyes suddenly sharpened and he turned quickly, grabbing the little man's arm in a hard grip. "You're damned right he'll be there waiting," he said. "You tryin' to tell us Cribbins would duck out?" His voice was ugly and Santino tried to pull away.

"Listen," Luder cut in. "For God's sake let's not start fighting now. We got enough problems. Don't worry about the boss—you know damned well he'll be up there waiting. What we got to do is start thinking about ourselves and how we can get back to town."

Mitty dropped the little man's arm and nodded sagely. "That's right," he said. "We gotta think about us. I'm for picking up a heap—quick."

Luder shook his head. "No," he said. "Too risky. Let's just split up and see what happens. Why don't one of you head for the depot and the other start out for the bus station. I'll take off for White Plains and get a train.

"Not me," Mitty said. "They'll be watchin' those depots and bus stops an' I'm known around this town. Don't forget, I worked here. The cops know me. I'll take my chances on a car."

"I don't like that train or bus idea either," Santino said. "I'm with Mitty. A car's best."

"Well, whatever we do," Luder said, "we gotta get started. We can't hang around here; this place will be hotter'n a pistol in no time at all."

"It's hot right now," Santino said. He, like the others, became aware of the far off wail of the police sirens.

Ten minutes later Luder and Santino slowly walked down a street a couple of blocks away. It was a quiet, middle-class residential street, all but deserted. They walked very slowly, watching a point half a block ahead where Mitty had found a car sitting at the curb. Mitty had passed the car once and he'd known immediately that given only two or three minutes undisturbed, he'd be able to get the engine started. They were almost opposite him when the police prowl car swung into the street at the corner. Luder saw it first and he reached out quickly and tapped Santino on the wrist.

"Cops," he said. "For Christ's sake keep on walking. Don't do anything but just walk, slow and easy. They won't be looking for a couple of guys out for a walk."

He spoke without moving his lips and looking straight ahead. It took iron control, but he didn't change pace. Once, however, his eyes darted across the street to where Mitty was working on the car.

Mitty himself had his back to the direction from which the police car was approaching and it was obvious that he was unaware of it. He leaned into the sedan, his hand up under the dashboard as he manipulated the wires. Luder wanted to warn him, but he had no time.

They had just passed Mitty when the police car screeched to a halt. Luder was in time to see Mitty look up, startled. And then the single cop in the car had leaped to the street, a gun in his hand.

They could hear Mitty's high-pitched voice as they continued down the street.

"That does it," Santino said, the moment they had turned the nearest corner. "That does it. Here's where you and I split. I'm taking a chance on the railway station. You do what you want. I'm headin' for the station."

"Okay," Luder said. "You try it that way. I'm going to hit the highway and see if I can hitchhike a ride. Whoever gets into town, if either of us make it, call Goldman. Tell him what happened; tell him they got Mitty."

Santino nodded and stepped out ahead of the other man.

"Don't try to contact the country," Luder called after him. "Just Goldman. Goldman will get hold of Harry."

Santino didn't bother to answer.

Luder slowed his pace until the other man had reached the next corner and turned into the cross street.

Cribbins waited until Paula had closed and locked the door and then he pulled his right arm out from under his coat. He stretched it a couple of times and then took the gun he held in his hand and carefully put in into the shoulder holster he wore under his left armpit.

Paula just stood there, her dark eyes wide with curiosity.

"Get me a drink," Cribbins said. "I need one."

Paula backed up a step and her eyes went to Joyce.

"For God's sake, Harry," she said, "what happened? And who's she?"

"I said get me a drink," Cribbins repeated. "We'll talk later." He turned toward Joyce. "You want a shot?"

Joyce shook her head. "No thank you," she said. She was aware of the fact that her voice sounded terribly dignified. If it hadn't been for the circumstances, she might have laughed. But she merely stood there, stiff and sick with fear, as the dark-haired girl went into another room and a moment later returned with a half-filled bottle of whisky and a glass.

Cribbins reached out and took the bottle from her hand. He didn't speak as he filled the glass a quarter of the way full and downed it in a single gulp.

"Okay," he said. "Now what can we do with her?" He nodded his head toward Joyce.

"Look, Harry," Paula said, "what happened? What's going on, anyway? Where's Santino and the boys? And who's the dame? I thought . . . "

"Don't think," Cribbins said. "Listen." He nodded toward Joyce. "We're keeping this little lady for a few days. Keeping her quiet and out of sight. Let's take care of her first and then we can talk. And don't worry about the boys; they're all right. I think we all better get upstairs. But there's one thing I want you to do first. You got a large shopping bag of some kind?"

Paula nodded her head, a baffled expression on her face

"Okay. Go out to the garage and open the trunk of that

Chevy we came in." He took a key out of his pocket and handed it to her. "Take out the chopper and put it in the bag and bring it into the house. Leave the rest of the stuff in the trunk. Lock it, and be sure to snap the padlock on the garage doors. Bring the chopper back to the house."

Paula hesitated, holding the key in her hand.

"Go on, do what I tell you," Cribbins said.

He waited until she had left the room and then he turned to Joyce. "Sit down," he said. "Sit down and listen to me."

Joyce edged over to a straight-backed chair.

"You're going to be here for a while," Cribbins said. "Several days at least. Make up your mind to it. Now you can have it just as easy or as rough as you want it. Nobody's to see you and you're to make no effort to get away. You get cute and you may force me to do something I don't want to do. On the other hand, you behave yourself, keep quiet and stay away from the windows and so forth, and you'll make it a lot easier for all of us."

Joyce stared at him dumbly for a moment or two and then swallowed a couple of times and spoke.

"My husband," she said. "He's going to know something has happened to me. Can't I just let him know that I'm . . ."

"You can't let anyone know anything. For the next few days you're out of circulation. Completely out of circulation. Make a bum move and we'll take you out for good."

At nine-fifteen on Monday evening, Paula came back downstairs, carrying the tray. Cribbins, sitting on the couch in the living room in his shirt sleeves, looked up as she hesitated a moment before putting it down on the sideboard.

"She still won't eat anything?"

Paula shrugged. "Just coffee," she said. "Says she's not hungry. Wanted to know if I didn't have something for the dog."

"The hell with the dog," Cribbins said.

Paula crossed over and threw herself down next to Cribbins, crossing her legs.

"Listen, Harry," she said, "do you think it's safe just leaving her up there locked in the room?"

"Sure it's safe. Why not? What do you expect her to

do? She's handcuffed, isn't she? The doors locked and you've taken her clothes."

"She can still scream," Paula said.

Cribbins looked at her, annoyed. "She's not a fool, Paula," he said. "I nailed those shutters on the inside; no one would hear her but us. And she knows what I'd do if she makes trouble. That girl's scared stiff, and as long as she remains that way, we won't have any trouble from her."

Paula looked up and gave him a long look. "What did you want to bring her here for anyway?" she asked. "My God, a woman and a dog!"

Cribbins turned on the couch and stared at her coldly. "Are you stupid?" he said. "I've told you; given you a diagram of the whole thing. What the hell did you expect me to do—turn her loose to start yelling for the cops? Let's stop worrying about her. Let's just think about us."

Paula pouted her lips and then lay back against the couch and shrugged.

"All right, Harry," she said, "let's start thinking about us. Do you know this is the first time you and I have ever been really alone? And speaking of that, don't you think it's about time we heard from the others? Someone should have called by now. How about Goldman; he must know what's going on. Why hasn't he called? I'm getting worried."

"Worrying isn't going to do any good," Cribbins said. "You heard the broadcasts; the cops haven't got anyone. The boys must have made it back to town. They're playing it smart and lying low. They'll be showing up, but probably not for another day or so. They'll have to get hold of a car and they'll have enough sense to wait until the heat dies down a little. There's no point in worrying; no point in borrowing trouble. Goldman will call; just give him time."

"Okay, Harry, I won't worry. Anyway, as far as that goes, it will be all right with me if they never show up. Especially Santino. I'll be happy if he drops dead."

As she spoke she shook her head, tossing the long black hair out of her eyes, and leaned over so that she rested against his shoulder.

"So here we are," she said.

"Yes—here we are."

His arm lifted and fell across her shoulders. She moved closer to him and then suddenly pulled back.

"Take that shoulder holster off, Harry," she said. "It isn't very comfortable."

Cribbins pulled away from her and got to his feet.

"Sure, Paula," he said. "I'll take it off, and I'll go out and mix us a drink. In the meantime you might make yourself more comfortable. Get out of that suit and into a housecoat or something. We won't be having any callers tonight, but I think I'll sit it out downstairs here, just in case. You want to stay down here with me, that'll be fine. But if we're going to sit it out, you better get yourself set for the night."

Paula half closed her eyes, watching him as he moved toward the kitchen. Then she slowly got up and stretched. She turned and climbed the stairs.

Cribbins was again sprawled out on the couch when she re-entered the room. He'd mixed a couple of drinks and they stood on the table in front of the couch.

Paula was wearing a wraparound terrycloth robe, her legs and feet bare. She stood for a moment in front of him and then suddenly threw herself down so that she fell across his lap.

He half pushed her away.

"What's the matter, Harry?" she said, her voice languorous, but without annoyance. "Nobody's coming—you said so yourself. Don't you like me, Harry? Don't you like women?"

"I like women," Cribbins said. "I like you, kid. But it's like I told you from the first. When I'm doing a job, the job comes first. I don't mix things."

"You just mixed a drink," Paula said. "And anyway, the job's done. Over and done with."

For a moment he looked at her. He felt tired; not sleepy, just tired. "You're right, kid," he said at last. "You're right. The job is over and done with."

He reached for her then and as she came to him the terrycloth robe fell open and he felt the firm, warm flesh of her body press against him as her arms went around his neck.

She kissed him and then pulled back her head and looked into his eyes. "That bastard Santino should be here now," she said. "He's the kind who likes to watch."

"We'll give him something to watch, then," Cribbins

said. "But let's do it in the dark." His hand reached up for the switch of the shaded lamp on the end table.

Once or twice the sound of the dog's barking drifted down from the floor above, but both of them were oblivious to it. It wasn't until the sharp double ring of the telephone reached their ears that they pulled away from each other.

Cribbins was off of the couch and switching on the light before the sound had ceased. "Get it," he said.

Paula got up slowly, a small, secret smile on her bruised, sensuous lips. She crossed the room, moving slowly. A moment later he heard her voice coming from the hallway, and almost before he could get to his feet she was back in the room.

"You better take it, Harry," she said. "I think it's Goldman."

He was several minutes on the phone and Paula strained her ears to listen. But Cribbins merely grunted once or twice, saying nothing after his original hello. Finally he replaced the receiver and came back into the living room. He reached down and took the half-filled glass which held the warm remains of his drink and downed it. He was frowning when at last he spoke.

"It was Goldman, all right," he said. "He's heard from the boys. The cops got Mitty. Picked him up while he was trying to snatch a car in Brookside."

"And the others?"

"They made it back to town. They're laying low."

Paula pulled the robe closer around her body and shook her hair out of her eyes. There was a worried, anxious expression on her face.

"Harry," she said, "let's get out of here. Let's blow. Right now." She looked at him with a sudden sly expression. "Come on, Harry," she said. "Just you and me. We've got the money—let's get out of here."

He looked at her speculatively, so that she knew he was considering it, considering everything. Then at last he hunched his shoulders and shook his head.

"Don't be a damned fool, kid," he said. "Don't go panicky and blow your top. So they got Mitty. So what? Mitty won't talk. Mitty is as safe as the Bank of England. No one saw him during the stickup except possibly the driver, and he's dead. The guy in the back of the truck was out like a light. No, Mitty will keep his mouth shut."

Paula stared at him and opened her mouth to speak, but he went on, not giving her a chance.

"No, it's more important than ever that we stay now," he said. "Mitty will never talk as long as he knows we're here waiting for him. No one saw Mitty, and Mitty is safe."

"No one saw Mitty," Paula said slowly, "except the girl. The girl upstairs. She saw all of you. Remember that, Harry. She saw all of you."

Cribbins nodded. "I'm remembering. Never fear, kid, I'm remembering."

6.

KARL MITTY was tired. Jees, it was funny what a couple of years of soft living could do to a guy. Funny how you could get out of shape so fast. He was dead tired; he could hardly keep his eyes open. Even with the bright light shining down into his face from the two-hundred-watt bulb, the hard, stiff chair under his buttocks and the occasional hard fist which was pushed under his chin to bring his face up, he still could hardly keep from closing his eyes and falling asleep.

My God, you'd think these guys would give up, that they'd get tired too. Except of course it wasn't the same guys. They kept shifting around; new ones coming in to replace the ones who had grown hoarse and drenched with sweat as they stood in a semicircle around him and aimed the questions, like stiff-armed punches, at his head.

He was tired, but really he had to laugh. Did they think that they could wear him down? Why, for Christ's sake, these guys were cream puffs. Soft bums who got silly in their heads from plush living. Karl Mitty had taken plenty in his day, and he could still take all these bums had to dish out—and then some. And they didn't have a thing on him, not one damned thing. He wasn't smart, but he could tell that by the questions they kept repeating over and over again.

He'd lost track of the time a long while back and of course down here in the concrete, windowless basement room, he was unable to tell whether it was night or day, but he guessed he must have spent at least twenty hours in this same chair. Except of course for that first interval, when the plainclothes cop with the deceptively pleasant manner had tried to make up to him and had taken him into the other room for the coffee and sandwiches. It hadn't gotten the guy anywhere, of course, any more than the tough ones had gotten anywhere with him.

There'd been that break and the other break when the small, thin cop in the eyeglasses had taken out the blackjack and had lost his temper and banged away at his neck while the other two held him. It had made him sick and he'd puked and so they'd let him up while they washed down the floor with a hose. The cops couldn't stand the smell of a little puke, for God's sake!

Yeah, he must have been here for a good twenty-four hours now and they'd got exactly nowhere with him, except to make him awfully tired.

He hadn't even admitted trying to steal the car. He might be dumb, but he was too smart for that. Sure, it would have been nice to have grabbed a plea and taken the small rap, but he knew that if he admitted it, he'd never make bail. If he didn't admit it, just stuck to his story that he was leaning against the car and tying his shoelace, sooner or later they'd have to give up. Sooner or later they'd charge him, but Goldman would be around with the bail bond money. It was just a case of hanging on and admitting nothing. He might be a little punchy, as they said he was, but he wasn't as crazy as they were if they thought they could make him crack.

He suddenly felt the cool damp rag on his forehead and he quickly snapped open his eyes again and jerked his head erect.

It was the nice cop again, the smart boy with the felt hat slanted across his brow who'd tried to play it cute and pretend to be his friend.

"All right, Mitty," the cop said. "You can take it easy now. I didn't know these guys had been keeping you down here all this time. Hell, I thought they'd taken you upstairs hours ago and booked you. They had no right keeping you down here this long. I'll tell you what, I'm going to send out and have a container of coffee and some food brought in and you eat them. While you're doing it, I gotta go upstairs for a few minutes and see the lieutenant. You eat and catch a little shut-eye and then, after a while, why I'll be back and maybe we can talk again, eh?"

Mitty stared at him and smiled crookedly.

"Sure, sure," he said. "We can talk. But like I told you, there ain't a thing to talk about. Nothin'."

Horace Sims, detective first grade, waited patiently until Lieutenant Parks finished with the telephone call. He stood over by the window, not bothering to remove his hat, and looked out, a bored expression on his heavy face.

Lieutenant Parks didn't look up as he flung the receiver back into its cradle. "I want you to go down and talk to him again," he said, annoyed. "It's just too damned much of a coincidence."

Sims nodded. "Right away. But can you spare a moment? It's about the Sherwood woman."

"About who?"

"The Sherwood woman. Remember—she's missing. You sent me out with her husband last night to look the house over."

Parks looked up, thoughtful for a moment. He had a lot on his mind. "What about her? Has she turned up yet?"

"No. But I've run into something a little odd."

"I thought you were back working on the Rumplemyer job," Parks said, irritated.

"I am. But I stopped out at the Sherwood house around noon because I happened to be in the neighborhood. He's been calling in all morning bothering us. I just stopped as I was passing—we covered everything I could think of last night. I'd suggested that Sherwood find out if his wife had drawn any money out of her bank. They have a joint account. It was just a routine suggestion. Well, it turns out she not only stopped at the bank after she took him to the train yesterday morning; she drew out just about every dime they had between them. Twenty-six hundred dollars, to be exact. Got a certified check made out to cash."

Parks drew down the corners of his thin, wide mouth and slowly nodded his head.

"So-o-o. Well, that should make the picture a lot clearer. She probably just got fed up with her marriage, or maybe had someone else on the string and took the money and blew."

Sims shook his head, turned away from the window, and stepped toward the desk.

"I don't think so," he said. "I talked with young Sherwood for more than an hour last night and I went over that house mighty carefully. There's no doubt that she never returned after taking him to the station, and the way the house was left, she certainly must have intended to come back to it. If she was going to leave him, take the dough and scram, why wouldn't she have gone back for her clothes? She had plenty of time.

"Another thing, I get the very strong impression, from talking with him and several of the neighbors, that they got along very well together. She doesn't seem to be at all the kind of woman who would have had anything going, on the side. Of course you can never tell, but I have a pretty strong feeling about it. Something has happened to her."

Parks nodded.

"What else makes you reach that conclusion?"

"Sherwood told me this noon that twice the telephone rang during the morning and each time when he picked up the receiver a man's voice asked for his wife. Same voice each time, he said. The guy hung up when Sherwood answered."

"*That* don't exactly sound as though she was so damned pure. You sure this guy Sherwood is leveling with you?" Parks asked.

"I'm never sure of anything. On the other hand, I'd bet he's on the up and up. And I don't like the idea of her disappearing with a certified check made out to cash."

For several seconds Parks sat in deep thought. Finally he looked up.

"Okay," he said. "I can't spare you right now with this damned Rumplemyer mess on our minds, but maybe you better stick with the Sherwood thing for another day or so. Go on out to the house again and see if you can find anything at all. Try and get a little better picture of the woman from the husband. Also, if that guy should call again, you pick up the phone and try and get a trace on the call. I'll go downstairs and take care of this mug Mitty."

"You think maybe you got something there, with him?"

The lieutenant shrugged. "Hell, I don't know," he said. "Probably just one of those damned coincidences, but we aren't passing up any bets. The guy used to be a driver for Rumplemyer. Worked there about six months back, for several weeks. Quit his job for no reason at all. Told them he couldn't handle the job because he had a bad back. Anyway, he has a record, all petty stuff. Used to be a prize-fighter at one time. Strictly third rate. Then he just drifted around, working now and then. In trouble a couple of times on assault charges, and once for larceny. Funny, his being picked up yesterday morning an hour after the stick-up, trying to steal an automobile. He was in the front seat and working on the wires when a squad car happened to pass. Murphy, who was driving, spotted him and made the arrest."

"Doesn't seem that a guy who has just finished pulling a quarter-million stickup would be hanging around trying to lift a hot car," Sims commented.

"It doesn't to me either," Parks admitted, "But it is a rather odd coincidence. Anyway, we don't seem to be getting anywhere with him. We can hold him for the car job, of course, but we'll have to charge him. The second we do, he can demand bail. And get it—unless we can tie him in on the other some way. Anyway, you stay with the Sherwood thing. I'll see Mitty. But try and wind it up. Missing wives are all well and good, but the commissioner is a damned sight more worried about missing money at this point. Missing money, and a dead man."

Sims grunted and turned to the door. "I'll keep in touch."

Goldman kept his eye on the traffic and drove slowly, heading north through the park and keeping the car at an even thirty miles an hour. He kept both hands on the steering wheel and didn't bother to remove the short cigar butt from the corner of his mouth as he talked. His heavy lips were stretched tight across his face and his eyes behind the thick-lensed glasses were hard and cold as he spoke. He never looked at the man at his side.

"You shouldn't have called me at the apartment," he said. "God damn it, how many times do I have to tell you guys. You wantta get hold of me, call the office. That's where I do business, out of the office."

Santino moved nervously on the leather seat of the car, shifting so that he seemed to squeeze his small body into the very corner. He too looked straight ahead as he talked. "I had to call you," he said. "It was important. Cribbins said to get hold of you the second I made town. I had to tell you about Mitty."

"God damn it," the lawyer said, "don't mention no names to me. I don't know no Mitty."

"Well, I had to let you know the cops got him. Cribbins wants you to get him out."

Goldman laughed bitterly. "So I should get him out! Are you all crazy? How the hell am I supposed to know that the cops got him, huh? You expect those cops up there to think I'm clairvoyant or something? Cribbins knows better and so should you. Mitty will call *me* as soon as he gets the chance. I can't call him. And don't worry, Mitty won't talk. Sooner or later he'll contact me. I represented him before so it's only natural."

"I suppose," Santino said sarcastically, "that the Brookside cops are just going to be real nice and give him a dime and he can call you and you can spring him."

Goldman shifted the cigar around in his mouth. "You happen to suppose just right," he said. "That's the trouble with all of you punks—you don't know you're alive. Of course the cops will let him call. They'll work him over, but sooner or later they'll let him make a call. After all, this ain't Russia. They'll let him call and when he does my office will get it and one of my boys will go up and get him out. Even Mitty is smart enough to know that."

"All right," Santino said. "The hell with Mitty. I'm not worrying about Mitty anyway. What I'm worrying about is me. What about me?"

"Well, what about you?" Goldman said. "What the hell do you expect me to do—drive you up there and hold hands with you? Good God, first you guys muff this whole thing —make a mess out of it and end up knocking off the driver. Then you haven't enough brains to make a clean getaway. What the hell do you want me to do? I'm a lawyer, not a baby-sitter."

Santino turned and looked at the man beside him with cold, bitter eyes. "Nuts," he said. "Don't con me, mister. I know who you are, and I ain't asking you for nothing. I only called last night because Cribbins told me to call you. And the only reason I'm seeing you today is because you were too cagey to talk over the phone and told me to see you. As far as I'm concerned, you ain't nothing. Nothing at all. But I did think, that knowing what happened, you might arrange a car so Luder and I could get up to the country."

"Why don't you rent a car?"

"I don't rent a car because I'm not stupid," Santino said. "For the same reason I don't take no bus nor no train. I was damned lucky I didn't get picked up when I caught that train into town from Brookside. Luder and I talked it over when we met last night and we figured it would be best if you could get us a car of some kind."

For the first time Goldman took his eyes off the road and turned to glance at the little man next to him.

"Brother," he said, "you *are* crazy. I should get you a car yet! And suppose you get picked up on suspicion. The car gets traced right smack back to me. That would be just great, wouldn't it?"

He hesitated for a minute and then continued. "I guess I got to do your thinking for you. The best thing is to lay low for at least another day. Then if you don't want to rent a car, or steal one, you'll have to borrow one. Borrow it from some friend or a cousin or something. You got a cousin or something, haven't you?"

Santino didn't answer.

"Where's Luder now, by the way."

"What's it matter?"

"It doesn't," the lawyer said. He drove on for several minutes in silence and then once more spoke.

"Look," he said, "don't get me wrong. It's just that I'm annoyed the way things turned out. This isn't my caper, you know. I told Harry that I'd handle the stuff after you got it, and that I'd represent you boys if there was any trouble. It isn't that I don't want to help you, but I have to watch my step. I'm a lawyer and a respectable businessman and I don't take chances."

"I'm not asking you to," Santino said.

"Then don't. As far as a car is concerned, I can let you have some dough if you're short. You'll have to work out the details yourself."

"I'm not short," Santino said crisply. "And I can get a car all right. I'll borrow one. You can drop me off anywhere. I'll grab a cab."

"I'll take you back to the bar where I picked you up. And you and Luder take it easy. I talked with Harry last night after I heard from you. He knows about Mitty, and there's nothing to worry about there. Just you and the old man take it easy and don't rush up to the country. Harry'll wait."

"Sure—sure," Santino said. "Why shouldn't he? He's got plenty of company. Two good-lookin' broads. Why shouldn't he wait?"

For a moment the lawyer looked startled and he slowed down for a traffic light and waited until it had changed before he again spoke. "What the hell do you mean, two broads?" he asked. "I thought that that girl of yours was up there alone."

Santino laughed without humor. "Yeah—two," he said. "My Paula, and the other one. The one he snatched when we pulled the job."

Goldman for the first time reached up and took the cigar out of his mouth. He pulled over to the curb and stopped and turned toward the other man.

"The girl he snatched?" he said in a hollow voice. "What in the name of Christ do you mean, the girl he snatched? What girl?"

Santino took his time telling about it, and enjoyed watching the blood leave the lawyer's sallow face and watching as his hands began to shake imperceptibly as he tried to get the cigar butt back between his lips.

For several minutes after the little man finished speaking, Goldman said absolutely nothing. Then at last he reached down and again started the car. He spoke once again when they were under way.

"That does it," he said. "That does it up just fine! A kidnaping—that's all we needed."

"It will have to be a little more than just a kidnaping," Santino said. "The girl was there when I used the chopper. She was there when it happened."

Bart Sherwood needed a shave. He also needed something a lot more substantial than the dozen cups of black coffee he had existed on during the last thirty-two hours. He'd finally managed a little rest early on Tuesday morning with the help of several sleeping tablets, but by seven o'clock he was up and nervously pacing the floor.

He put the coffee on, started to open the refrigerator and get out the bowl which held the eggs. But there was something about the kitchen, with the dirty dishes still there from the previous morning, which brought a lump to his throat. This was Joyce's job, making the breakfast. Something she always did. Suddenly he had no desire for food. He'd just have coffee and let it go at that.

He walked into the bathroom, and there, at the edge of the black-tiled sink, was the twisted tube of toothpaste, with the cap off, where she had left it in her hurry to prepare his breakfast and get ready to take him to the station. It was one of those little things which they had fought over a hundred times, but somehow this morning, instead of the sense of irritation he had always experienced, he felt a constriction in the region of his heart.

Carefully he picked up the tube, found the cap and screwed it back on. He forgot about brushing his own teeth. The bathroom was like the kitchen. It reminded him of Joyce. She was everywhere in the house; in the empty bed, in the living room, everywhere.

God, what *could* have happened to her?

He took a wet washcloth and wiped his face and went back to the kitchen and downed two cups of black coffee. At nine o'clock he called his office and said he wouldn't be in. He didn't explain; he couldn't. How do you go about telling your secretary that your wife is missing?

God knows the news would be around soon enough. He knew that the papers would pick up the story, especially if foul play were suspected. Normally the thought of the publicity would have bothered him, but by now he was long past the stage of being bothered by anything so trivial. He didn't care what happened, just so Joyce was found and Joyce was all right.

The newspaper was outside the door and the idea of possible publicity made him go out and get it. It was a New York morning paper and he looked through it carefully. There was plenty about the robbery of the Rumplemyer armored car out in Brookside and about the murder of the driver, but there was nothing about a missing girl named Joyce Sherwood.

Maybe missing wives weren't news, after all.

Thank God, there were things to be done. To him they seemed futile, rather ridiculous things, but the detective who'd accompanied him home the previous evening had suggested he do them. Although they didn't seem to make much sense, he'd follow the man's instructions to help fill in the time. Anything was better than just pacing the floor and waiting.

He looked into the file of old bills and found the receipt for repairs on Joyce's watch. He called the jeweler, and the jeweler gave him the serial number of the watch. Bart wrote it down and then telephoned it in to the police station, giving it to the desk clerk with a request that he give Sims the information.

Next he looked up the slip of paper which had the number of Flick's dog license. He telephoned the pound and reported the dog missing and gave them a description and the license number.

He notified the insurance company that the car was missing. For a moment, when they asked if it was stolen, he hesitated. He didn't know what to say. How can you say your wife has stolen your car? But Sims had said to report it. He ended up by saying he thought so.

He was about to telephone the bank and was looking the number up when the first call came from a man whose voice he didn't recognize. The man asked for Mrs. Sherwood and for a second he fought to catch his breath.

"She's out," he said at last, in almost a whisper. "This is Mr. Sherwood."

The click of a receiver being replaced on its hook struck his eardrum.

He was still wondering about the call when he finally telephoned the bank. That's when he learned about the certified check. For a moment or so he just sat there, wordless with shock.

"Are you sure?" he asked at last.

The bank was sure. He wasn't satisfied and insisted on speaking to the teller who had waited on her. He had to believe him. There couldn't be any doubt at all about it. The man even remembered the conversation; how he had warned Mrs. Sherwood that carrying a certified check was just like carrying cash.

Detective Sims had stopped by at noon, just casually, saying he was in the neighborhood. Bart told him what he had learned. It embarrassed him somehow, but he'd also told Sims about the man who'd called and asked for his wife and then hung up; and about the second call, from the same man, a few minutes before noon, when the same thing had happened.

It was after this telephone call that Bart walked into the living room and over to the liquor chest and portable bar which Joyce had given him for Christmas. Neither of them drank much, but now and then Bart would bring home people from the office and she knew that he took a particular pride in his mixed drinks. He'd been pleased with the liquor chest; it was the sort of extravagance neither of them would ever have indulged in on normal occasions, but Christmas was in no way a normal occasion and they went out of their way to get each other the sort of things which they considered "extravagances."

Joyce had insisted that Bart take the key to the liquor chest and keep it on his chain with his other keys, and this had pleased him immeasurably for some odd reason.

He found the key now and opened the chest. A moment later he took out an unopened bottle of Scotch, one which had also been given to him by someone at the office at Christmas. He opened the bottle, having trouble with the metal cap, and found a shot glass and filled it. Then he took the drink and walked over to the big armchair in which he always sat in the evenings. He left the bottle uncapped, sitting on top of the liquor chest, the doors swinging open.

For a while he just sat there, holding the glass. At last he sighed and lifted it and drank it, making a wry face as the liquid hit his all but empty stomach.

God, it seemed utterly impossible that you could live with a person, know them and love them and share your every thought and feeling with them, for a year—and still not know them at all. His mind was in a turmoil and he knew that he wasn't really thinking very clearly, but the fact remained that certain things were inescapable.

Joyce was gone. Joyce had been at the bank, she'd taken twenty-six hundred dollars out of their account in the form of a certified check, and then she had vanished. After she had last been seen, in the bank, anything might have happened to her. She could have been in an accident, she could have been kidnaped—although this seemed utterly fantastic—or she might have been stricken with amnesia. But one single, clear fact stood out above all others: she had been perfectly normal when she had dropped him off at the railway station; she had apparently been completely normal when she had appeared at the bank to make the withdrawal.

And the man who had called twice on the telephone and hung up each time when Bart had answered.

For the first time since she had disappeared, Bart Sherwood had a momentary doubt about his wife. Was it conceivable that there was another man? Was it possible that she had taken the money and run away?

He stood up suddenly, shaking his head angrily at his own thoughts. It wasn't possible. He knew full well that no person ever completely understands any other person; knew that no one really knows another's heart. But he couldn't so completely have misjudged and misunderstood her.

There was a reason somewhere. The money could be explained, and so could the telephone calls. It was possible that she had withdrawn the money, possible that by the most fantastic stretch of the imagination she might have some other man in her life. It was even possible that she could have taken the money and run off with this other man.

But it was utterly and completely impossible that she could have done it in this way, without first telling him about it. On that he would stake his life.

There had to be some explanation, some plan in back of the whole thing.

At two o'clock the doorbell rang and he crossed the living room, throwing the door open quickly, hoping . . .

His face fell when he saw Sims standing there, leaning against the side of the door jamb.

"Have you . . ." he began.

Sims shook his head and stepped inside.

"Nothing yet," he said. "I'm sorry, but nothing . . ."

They sat down and Sims again began the questions, the thousand and one questions.

It infuriated him; he wanted to hit the man. But in the back of his mind he realized that Sims was, in his way, trying to help him, doing his job the way he saw it. He hadn't minded so much when, from the tenure of the questions, it seemed the detective had a vague idea in the back of his mind that he, Bart Sherwood, might have some guilty knowledge. It was ridiculous, but Bart knew that a good cop should investigate every angle, suspect everyone. And he wanted a good cop on the job.

The thing which irritated him was the other line of questioning. Who had Joyce known before their marriage? Had she been engaged or gone out with other men? Did she have any particular male friends? What was the matter with Sims? Good God, what kind of girl did he think she was?

And the business about the money. He had no answers to that. No answers at all. He could see what was in back of the detective's mind, and understood what he might be thinking.

"I just don't know," he said helplessly. "I just don't know. I have no explanation. It seems impossible . . ."

Then the telephone rang again and as Bart started to get up, Sims quickly shook his head.

"Let me," he said.

Bart stared at him as he crossed the room. Lifting the receiver from the hook, the detective held his hand half over his mouth. He spoke in a nasal, sing-song voice, a voice with a Southern accent.

"Miss Sherwood's residence," he said.

He listened for a moment and then spoke again.

"Miss Sherwood stepped out fo' a few minutes. Nobody heah but me—ah'm the window cleaner. You wanna leave a message?"

He looked over at Bart, his eyes suddenly widening. He nodded quickly, then slowly put the receiver back.

"What was it?"

Sims looked thoughtful for a second and then answered. "It just could be the same man who called before," he said. "He didn't give me his name, but he did give me a number." He was scribbling on a notebook as he finished.

"I'll get a trace," he said.

Fifteen minutes later the two men left the house. They used Sims's car and the detective drove fast, using his siren to run the red traffic lights.

7.

SHE COULD SEE the thin cracks of light filtering into the room through the closed wooden blinds and she knew that the room itself must face to the east. Some time during the early hours of the morning she must have finally fallen asleep because now it was daylight and now she was awake. Awake and lying on a bed in a strange room in a strange house.

With the realization that it was a new day came almost immediately her consciousness of the dull heavy pain in her arms and unthinkingly she started to turn onto her back. It was then she remembered that her wrists had been locked together by the handcuffs. The thin flannel blanket which they had thrown across her almost nude body had slipped during the night and lay half off the bed.

In spite of her knowing that she was alone in the room, her near nakedness embarrassed her and she struggled with her locked hands to bring the blanket back over her. It was the dark-eyed girl who had taken her clothes, had stripped her down to the diaphanous, transparent slip. She was becoming fully awake now, having first remembered the handcuffs and then the girl. Swiftly her mind recaptured the lost hours and it seemed incredible that this must be Tuesday morning and that all which had happened had taken place within the span of a single day.

Her eyes became accustomed to the dim light of the room and once more she gazed curiously around her. There was something almost pathetically incongruous about the room with its high, decorated ceiling, the faded, rich wallpaper and the beautifully parqueted floor; the room held nothing but the bare iron bed upon which she lay and the card table set up over against the wall. She knew that at one time this must have been one of the master bedrooms in a fine Victorian mansion and that traces of its former grandeur were still about her.

Flick, the poodle, lay in a ball at the end of her bed and he hadn't moved when she first awakened, but now he slowly stretched and leaped to the floor, straight-legged and yawning. He saw that her eyes were open and he moved over to her, his tail wagging furiously, waiting for her usual morning caress.

She spoke to him softly and he at once leaped back on the bed and snuggled close to her. . . .

Joyce Sherwood was a woman who'd had but a limited experience in life; in many ways she could be considered naive and unsophisticated. But at this moment she was fully aware of everything that had happened to her; fully understood the situation in which she found herself. She knew that she was not the victim of a kidnaping, in the normal sense of that word. She was not being held as a hostage. She had been unfortunate enough to have been at the wrong place at the wrong time; she had witnessed a robbery and a murder. She represented danger to the men who had committed those crimes.

It was a line of thought which she would have preferred not to pursue, but the implications were inescapable. She knew that if she were freed and the men later taken prisoners, she'd be the key witness who could put them in the death house. They had already committed one murder, so they had nothing to lose by committing a second if it would in any way enhance their safety. She couldn't avoid shivering as she thought about it. The only surprising thing was that she was still alive, and the fact that she was gave her the only source of possible hope.

There was a foul taste in her mouth and now she was hungry and slightly sorry she hadn't eaten when they had offered her food the night before. She began to wonder if they were up yet. Then she began to think again of what had happened, trying to remember every detail.

There had been four of them, and she knew from their conversation that they intended to meet again. Could that be what they were waiting for, why they hadn't done anything to her yet?

Once more she realized the way her thoughts were traveling and she made an effort to think of something else. She realized the futility of frightening herself by allowing her imagination to run wild. And so she tried to think of Bart and what Bart would be doing now. He must have reported her missing. He, and the police, must have realized that something had happened to her. Perhaps he had learned of the money she had drawn from the bank and if he had, the knowledge would be of no help. It would only serve to further confuse him. God, there must be some way . . .

Then she remembered the roadblock and the state trooper who had stopped their car as they'd driven north to the hide-out. He had asked for her driving license, read her name and her description, he had checked the license plates on her car.

She had a sudden revival of hope. They would find her, they had to. Bart would report her missing and the police would know about her and sooner or later they would find her. She must hang on to her senses, control her fears and her emotions and wait. It was only a question of time.

But in the back of her mind, as she tried to reassure herself, was the nagging bit of knowledge that the other members of the gang would be arriving, that time itself was running out.

There were footsteps outside of the door in the hallway and a moment later the door was pushed open. It was the girl with the dark eyes and the dark hair, and she was holding a tray in her hand. Flick looked up and barked.

"Hang on to that dog," the girl said.

Santino and Luder arrived at the house in Cameron Corners just before dark Tuesday evening. They came in a Ford station wagon which belonged to a friend of Santino, who'd loaned him the car for a few days with the understanding that Santino was not to use it for transporting narcotics or other illegal purposes.

It is a coincidence that the only person who noticed their arrival at the old three-story white house should have been Miss Bertha Abernathy.

Bertha Abernathy was a very nosy character, and the first to admit as much.

"Why shouldn't I be curious?" Miss Abernathy would ask if one of her friends should laughingly accuse her of being an indefatigable gossip and busybody. "My father and my grandfather were born here in Cameron Corners, and I've lived here all of my life. This is my home, my town. If anything happens around here, I like to know about it. Not, of course," she would add, "that very much does happen."

Cameron Corners is the sort of town in which just about anything, from the arrival of a new family to a high-school basketball game, is big news. There is no local newspaper to report these events, but the town doesn't really need a newspaper. The town has Miss Abernathy, who, now that she's retired as librarian, has all her time to devote to her avocation and hobby.

It was only natural, when she looked out her living-room window and saw the station wagon turn into the driveway of the place across the way, that she should be curious. Miss Abernathy's family and the Bleekses had been close friends for longer than she cared to remember. She'd been brought up with Aggie Bleeks and at one time it had been expected that she would be married to young Carlton Bleeks. But Carlton had been killed in World War I and the rest of the Bleekses had died off, all except Aggie, who had married an Italian count and moved to the Riviera. That had been more than ten years ago, and the old Bleeks mansion had been vacant for almost a decade, until it had finally been rented by a New York real estate agent this last spring. Aggie must have made the arrangements from her home in the Riviera, and Miss Abernathy had resented the fact that she hadn't written to her first about it. The young couple who'd taken the house were certainly queer ones. People by the name of Brown; a thin wisp of a man in his early thirties, who was almost never at home, and his rather common, though very pretty young wife.

Miss Abernathy had called, as she called on all new people who moved into the town, or at least the right part of the town, and had found the wife home alone. It hadn't been a very satisfactory call.

Mrs. Brown had a most peculiar accent and an almost psychopathic reserve, and her clothes were as odd as the furnishings which they had moved into the old place. Miss Abernathy saw only the living room, but that was plenty. The stuff looked as though it had come out of a Sears catalogue, which as a matter of fact, it had.

Miss Abernathy's call had not been returned, and although she was a little resentful, it really didn't bother her. The Browns were very strange people. It seemed that Mr. Brown was some sort of salesman and spent the week in New York. They never seemed to go out, never had visitors. It was because of this that Miss Abernathy had been most interested in seeing the station wagon arrive on that Tuesday just after dark. It was the second time in two days that the Browns had had company. Miss Abernathy already knew about the previous guests. She had been watching at the window on Monday afternoon when the girl and the odd-looking dog and the man with one arm drove into the old barn and then walked back down the driveway to enter the side door.

It was very strange. That very morning, Monday, she had met Mrs. Brown down at the market while she was shopping and had stopped to pass the time of day. Mrs. Brown had dropped the information that she was expecting guests—she'd been doing some rather heavy shopping from the size of the bags of groceries the clerk was piling into her car—and Miss Abernathy had commented on it.

"Mr. Brown is bringing some men home with him for a few days. Business acquaintances," Mrs. Brown had said.

She hadn't mentioned a dog and a woman and a man with one arm. And Mr. Brown hadn't been with the others when they arrived. There was something very odd about it, and it didn't take Miss Abernathy long to let her curiosity get the better of her. She paid a visit that afternoon.

Mrs. Brown almost hadn't let her in. But Miss Abernathy was an old hand at that sort of thing and she'd managed to push herself past the other woman into the parlor. There was no sign of the visitors.

Before she'd left, Mrs. Brown had explained. She almost had to, the way Miss Abernathy put her questions.

"My father," Mrs. Brown had said, "has been very ill and has come for a visit. His nurse accompanied him. He never goes anywhere without her. I know he would like to meet you, but he's upstairs resting."

"It's so nice you can have him," Miss Abernathy said. "But a shame it had to be just at this time."

"A shame?" The woman looked positively alarmed.

"Well, I mean of course when you were expecting your other guests. The men you told me were going to be here with your husband . . ."

"Oh, yes. Yes, of course."

Miss Abernathy had left soon afterward, but not before finding out that the dog belonged to the nurse and that Mrs. Brown's father would be around for an indefinite stay. She thought it was most peculiar—a nurse with her own dog. It couldn't be very good for a sick man.

And now Mr. Brown was back home and he had one of his guests with him. She watched the two men as they parked the car in the old barn in back of the house and returned to the side door. She imagined Mr. Brown would get a bit of a surprise when he found his father-in-law staying with them.

They certainly were strange people.

"Get rid of that damned dog!"

It was the slender dried-up one, the one with peculiar eyes, who was talking. The bony fingers of his nervous, clawlike hands incessantly played with each other as he sat across the room from her, in the overstuffed chair. His emaciated, evil face jerked on the scrawny neck in an oddly savage way as he emphasized his remarks, indicating the dog which sat still and alert at her feet.

Joyce was downstairs now, in what had been the parlor of the old mansion. They'd brought her down, after allowing her to get dressed, soon after the others had arrived.

"They wanna ask you some questions," the girl had told her. But they hadn't asked questions. They'd just talked among themselves. They were all there, all but the girl. She was probably preparing the evening's meal.

There was Cribbins, the one who had forced her at gunpoint to drive to the house. He was over on the couch under the drawn shades of the window and he was in his shirt sleeves. There was a cigarette in his thin, hard mouth and he'd removed his shoes and sat in his stocking feet. The gun which he never seemed to be without was strapped to his chest, and he wore the holster under his left arm-pit.

Next to him was the third man, the one who had arrived with the slender man. They called him Luder, and he was the only one who seemed even partially human. He was a big man, slightly gone to seed. He didn't speak at all; only the other two talked. The horrible part of it was the way they went on speaking to each other as though she weren't there in the room with them at all.

It was this cold indifference to her, more than anything else, which frightened her the most: the complete lack of reticence with which they discussed their plans—get rid of the dog. Would they go on from there? Would the next thing be: Get rid of the girl?

Joyce Sherwood shuddered and for a moment she almost lost the iron control which she had been exerting in an effort to fight off hysteria.

"We can't," Cribbins said. "It's too late for that."

The others looked at him quickly.

"Too late?"

"Yeah. Some old busybody across the street saw us arrive. She came over to see Paula and Paula gave her a song and dance. But she saw the dog. I don't want to do anything now to create curiosity. Anyway, we won't be here long. The heat's bound to die down within a few days. Then we can blow."

"The dog won't cause any trouble," Luder said. "He won't be talking to anyone."

"Anything can cause trouble," Santino snarled. He looked at Joyce and then his eyes went to the dog.

She felt the hidden menace in his words.

"We're all right just as long as we sit tight," Cribbins said. "We just can't do anything now to create suspicion. People know I'm here. They know she's here—" his head nodded to where Joyce sat. "We just have to lay low and sit it out for another few days. By that time Mitty should show. I can contact Goldman, and then we can blow. The way we planned it."

"You think Mitty is going to be okay?" Luder asked.

Cribbins shrugged. "How do I know?" he said. "You can bet he won't crack. The cop doesn't live who can make him talk. And they got nothing on him. Just an attempt to steal the car. He was stupid about that—but he won't talk."

"And suppose they keep on holding him?"

"He'll make bail. Sooner or later he's got to. He'll have been in touch with Goldman. He'd know enough to do that, once they let him get to a phone. And Goldman will spring him. Don't worry about Mitty."

"I worry about everything," Santino said. Once more he looked at Joyce out of his yellow, jaundiced eyes.

Cribbins stood up and stretched. "You worry too damned much," he said. "Come on, we'll go and get some grub. Paula will have something ready."

He walked to the door of the room and then turned back. "You stay here," he said to Luder. "Keep an eye on things. I'll have Paula bring you something."

Santino followed him out of the room and Luder went to the door and closed it after him. Joyce watched him with wide, frightened eyes. He seemed to feel her eyes on him and turned to her and half smiled.

"Don't fret, lady," he said. "I'm not going to hurt you." He tried to make it reassuring.

"What are they going to do with me?"

Joyce's words came in a tight whisper.

He dropped his eyes and half turned away. "Don't worry," he repeated. "Just don't make any trouble. Do what you're told to do." He wanted to change the subject. "That's a cute pup," he said. "A real cute dog. I had a dog a little while ago myself," he added, almost as an afterthought.

He held out his hand and snapped his fingers.

"You say his name's Flick? That's a good name for a poodle." He hesitated a second and then said, rather aimlessly, "You know, I'm a family man myself."

Once more he snapped his fingers at the dog. "I'll take him for a walk after we eat," he said.

Lieutenant Parks waited until Sims finished speaking, and then sat for several minutes before looking up. When he did, he looked directly at Bart Sherwood.

"I'd give it to the papers," he said slowly. "You got nothing to lose and it might help. I'm sorry about that other thing. When Sims tipped me off about the phone call, I thought we might have something. Thought it might help."

"Well, it helps this much," Sims said. "We know why

she drew out the twenty-six hundred dollars." He looked at Bart. "We know she was planning to surprise you with a new car for your birthday. We know that she didn't disappear voluntarily, anyway."

"I knew that all along," Bart said. "My God, I told you . . ."

"We have to make sure," Parks said, his voice conciliatory. "You're positive this guy Hartwell was telling the truth?"

Sims spoke up quickly. "I'm sure," he said. "You should have seen his face when we caught up with him after tracing the call. He explained why he hung up on Mr. Sherwood like he did. He said Mrs. Sherwood told him the car was to be a surprise birthday present and that naturally, when she didn't show to take delivery, he called up to see if she'd changed her mind. When Mr. Sherwood answered he didn't give his name for fear it would tip off the surprise. No, his story stands up all right."

Parks played with the letter opener on his desk and looked thoughtful. At last he shook his head and looked up. "Well, as I say, I think we better give it to the press. Tell them that we suspect foul play."

He held up his hand as Bart started to speak.

"I know," Parks said. "I know. I hate to worry you, hate even to suggest anything could have happened. But if we give it to them that way, at least they'll use it. Play it up. It may turn up some kind of a lead. Right now we have absolutely nothing at all to go on. Nothing. Publicity may not be pleasant, but we have to try to turn up something. Maybe your wife got amnesia. Maybe she—well I don't know what could have happened, but maybe someone or other saw her. Someone must have seen her. A woman and dog and a car just can't simply disappear. If the newspapers give the story a play, it might possibly help."

Bart nodded miserably. "God knows I want to try anything at all which will find Joyce," he said.

"We'll do everything we can. I know it's stupid of me to say so, but just try to hang on to yourself, try not to worry, try and get some . . ."

The ringing of the telephone interrupted him and he quickly reached for the instrument. He listened for several seconds and then put the receiver back on the hook.

"They sprung Mitty on bail," he said. "Not that it matters, I guess. One more day like this . . ."

Sims walked over and put his hand on Bart's shoulder. "You better go on home and get some rest," he said. "I'll take care of the newspapers."

Bart looked up at him dumbly. "Maybe if I offered a reward—" he began and then he suddenly realized that there was no money for a reward. All the money in the world which he and Joyce had was in a certified check which she carried with her. He hoped to God she still had it with her. He didn't want to think about what might have happened to her if she didn't.

Fifteen minutes later Bart Sherwood slowly walked away from the Brookside police station. He didn't wear a hat and his hair was disheveled. His necktie was loose at his throat and his shoulders were sagging, giving him the appearance of an old man.

It was after ten o'clock, on Wednesday evening. Joyce Sherwood had been missing for more than sixty hours.

A couple of miles to the south, in a small, one-story development house on which there was still a mortgage of more than seventy per cent of its outrageous sale price, a sad-faced woman sat with her two young children and tried to fight back the flow of tears which periodically drowned her rather pretty, soft, dark eyes. Her husband, Red Kenny, one time armored-car driver, had been dead for two days.

Wednesday was the day Flick disappeared, and it was also the day when Santino and Cribbins had their showdown. . . .

It was the business about Paula which probably planted the germ which was to grow rapidly and spread until the ultimate explosion came.

They'd argued about the money, down there in the kitchen after Joyce had been returned to her room and locked in. The three of them sat around the table and Paula had wanted to stay, but they'd sent her to the front part of the house on the pretext that they wanted her near the door in case anyone came.

It was Santino who'd insisted they bring the three canvas bags into the house and check the contents. Cribbins had argued against it, saying first that they should do nothing until Mitty arrived. He lost that argument, but he'd gone on to insist that no division should be made until the money had been exchanged for the bills which Goldman was bringing up. But Santino had insisted.

"Divide it now," he said. "What difference does it make? You can hold out Mitty's share. When Goldman comes, we just each turn over our individual shares. But it should be counted and divided now, in case something should happen and we should have to lam suddenly."

Luder was on Cribbins's side, of course, but they had finally given in rather than risk a fight over it.

That was the first thing and it had angered Cribbins, even though he privately admitted to himself that Santino had logic on his side. But he had shrugged it off and given in and the money had been brought into the kitchen and the bags opened. It had taken a long time to count it.

The loot totaled something over two hundred and thirty-eight thousand dollars. The trouble began then.

"As long as you insist," Cribbins said, "we'll cut it up. Three-tenths to me, the way we agreed. Two-tenths to each of you and to Mitty and one-tenth to Paula for arranging the hide-out."

"Put her tenth in with mine," Santino said.

Cribbins, who'd been arranging the bills, stopped, his hands still on the table, and looked at the other man.

"That's right," Santino said. "Paula's cut and mine together. I'll handle hers."

Cribbins slowly shook his head. "No, not that way. We give her her cut the way we arranged. What she does with it after we split out is her own business. But we said she gets one-tenth and she's going to get it."

Luder coughed and covered his mouth and then spoke, his voice conciliatory. "It doesn't matter, Harry," he said. "If Santino wants to take care of his girl's dough, what the hell—it doesn't matter."

"It matters a lot," Cribbins cut in, his voice cold and hard. "It matters a hell of a lot. Paula is in on this thing. She knows all about it. When we break out of here, I want to leave knowing that she's satisfied. I want to be damned sure everybody's happy when we split out."

He looked across the table at Santino, who slumped in his chair, his face twitching and his lean fingers nervously playing a tattoo on the edge of the table.

"As I say, what she does with it after she gets it is her own business—but I'm going to see that she gets it."

Santino began to nod his head slowly. His thin cheeks

were drawn in tight and his lips were pale and quivered slightly when he spoke. "What's all this sudden interest in Paula?" he asked. "You wouldn't be tryin' to take over, would you, by any chance?"

Slowly Cribbins drew his hands away from the money. He took a cigarette from the package on the table and deliberately took his time in lighting it. When he spoke his voice was smooth and barely audible.

"Listen, you little ape," he said. "Listen to me closely. You haven't got your chopper now, so just sit still and listen. If I wanted Paula, I'd take her. Any time, from anybody. Get that straight. And get something else straight —I don't happen to want her. I don't want any wet deck from you, or anything else you got."

Santino's right hand darted toward his trouser pocket, but Luder, sitting next to him, moved with amazing speed for an old man.

"All right, kid," he said, his hand grabbing Santino's wrist. "All right, just take it easy. You started this."

"I'll finish it," Santino said.

Cribbins suddenly leaned back in his chair and once more his hands rested easily on the table. Unexpectedly, he laughed.

"For God's sake, kid," he said. "What the hell are we fighting about? To you, the girl's a piece of merchandise. Why kid us about it? You'd let her go for a fifty-dollar bill, so why get serious about it? What you're worried about is the dough that comes with her. Get one thing straight in your head—I don't want that dough. I'm in this thing for my three-tenths and I'm going to be perfectly satisfied with that. The only thing is, we agreed that Paula would get a tenth for her part. I told you I don't give a damn what she does with it. She can keep it or she can turn it over to you, but I want to see that she gets it. I'm just trying to protect all of us. You may think you can control her, but I don't think any dame can be controlled. Not forever. So I don't want her thinking we screwed her on her cut on this job. I don't want her unhappy and talking. If you're as smart as I think you are, you'll handle it the same way."

Luder felt the little man relax and he removed his hand from his wrist.

"It's what we agreed on," he said. "Harry's right. He don't want your dame; he just wants to play it safe."

Santino stared at first one man and then the other. Slowly he leaned back in his chair. He took a cigarette from his pocket and before putting it into his mouth, coughed and then turned his head and spit into the corner.

"Oke," he said. "We won't argue. Do it your way." He looked up at the ceiling then, apparently losing interest in the matter. "Let's divvy it up," he said.

Dividing the money into five piles, Cribbins wrapped up each stack of bills with twine and put a slip on it, marked with their individual initials. Then he drew a long breath and leaned back in his seat.

"Call Paula in," he said.

Santino made no move, so after a moment, Luder got up and went to the front of the house. Cribbins looked down at his watch and saw that it was well after midnight.

Paula followed Luder back into the room and stood by the doorway, her eyes on the bundles of money.

"It's divided up," Cribbins said, "just the way we planned, only we've made the divvy now instead of waiting for Goldman. That's just in case anything should happen; in case we have to take it on the lam."

He reached down and took a suitcase from under the table. "I'm putting the money in here, where it's going to stay until Mitty and Goldman show. If everything goes right, we redivide, the same way, as soon as Goldman makes the exchange. But if anything should happen, grab the pile with your name on it and everyone is on his own." Carefully he tucked the money into the suitcase and closed it as the others watched. "I'm putting the keister in the closet up at the head of the stairs," he said.

He stood up and yawned.

"I want you to spend the night with the dame upstairs, Paula," he said. "We all should be getting some sleep."

Santino looked up then. "Why should she stay with the dame?" he said.

"It's better someone stays with her," Cribbins said. "I don't expect any trouble, but we'll all be sleeping and it's better someone stays in the room with her."

"So maybe I'll stay with her then," Santino said.

Paula suddenly laughed.

He was up like lightning and before either Luder or Cribbins could move, he crossed the room and viciously slapped her across the mouth. He was taking a second swing when Cribbins reached him.

"What the hell's the matter with you, anyway," he said. "You seem to want trouble."

Paula had fallen back and she was staring at Santino.

"You dirty little bastard," she said.

Cribbins half pushed her, turning her toward the doorway. "Do what I say, Paula," he said. "Go on upstairs and stay with that girl. And for God's sake let's not have any more arguments tonight."

Paula turned wordlessly and left the room.

"That bitch," Santino muttered. "Wait till this is all over. I'll fix her. I'll fix her, but good."

"Aw, let's cut it out and get some sleep," Luder said. "Where do we hit the deck, Harry?"

"It's safer to stay downstairs, in case of trouble," Cribbins said. "There's a couple of cots in the dining room—that's the room next to the living room. I'm going to have a cup of coffee and then hit the deck on the couch in the parlor."

"And about that . . ." Santino looked at the suitcase sitting on the edge of the table.

"Take it up and put it into the closet," Cribbins said, nodding at Luder.

8.

JOYCE had lain awake listening and when the single chime struck for the second time, she knew that it was one o'clock, Wednesday morning. Joyce turned over on her side —they'd changed the routine and now her wrist was handcuffed to the side rail of the bed so that she was slightly more comfortable and could sleep in more than one position. She used her free hand to pull the thin blanket up higher and closed her eyes, trying to fall asleep. It wasn't more than a minute or two later that Flick growled deep in his throat and then, as she heard the key in the lock of the door, the growl changed to a series of sharp barks.

The door opened and the girl Paula spoke soothingly to the dog. Joyce made no move, pretending sleep.

She heard the door close, and realized that although the girl had entered the room, she had not locked the door behind herself. A moment later she could hear Paula talking softly to the dog. Paula spoke then, turning toward the bed.

"I'm taking him downstairs," she said. "He's going to stay with old man Luder for the night. I'll be back—I'm spending the night up here."

Joyce didn't answer her.

The girl returned within minutes and again when she entered the room, she neither locked the door after herself nor did she turn on the light.

There were soft rustling sounds and Joyce knew that the other girl was stripping off her clothes.

"If you're going to be here," Joyce said, speaking very low, "I wish you would take off this handcuff. My wrist is sore where it's rubbed against it and my arm is cramped. I can't sleep."

Paula sat on the edge of the bed. "Are you nuts?" she said. "Why, they'd murder me if I did. Suppose you tried to get out or something?"

"I'm not going to try anything," Joyce said. "What chance would I have?"

"None," said Paula, flatly. "None at all." She hesitated a moment then and yawned. "All right," she said, "I'll unlock it. But you stay on the inside of the bed and don't try anything. Get smart and you'll get us both killed."

"I won't try anything," Joyce said.

There was a movement and then Paula struck a match. She found the key in the bag she'd carried into the room and a moment later she had the handcuff unlocked. She left it dangling at the side of the bed and seconds later had rounded the bed and crawled under the covers. Joyce sensed that she was completely naked. She was about to say good night when Paula spoke.

"Now go ahead and go to sleep," she said. "An' if you wake up first, wake me so I can get that cuff back on you."

The chimes which struck on the hour and half-hour rang out twice more before Joyce finally fell asleep.

Cribbins had taken the bottle of whisky and poured a shot into the cup of black coffee. He was sipping it when Luder returned to the kitchen. The older man carefully closed the door behind him as Cribbins watched him, an expression of inquiry on his thin, almost esthetic face.

"He's out like a light," Luder said. "The dog is in with him, tied up to the leg of the table."

"He take another one?"

"Yeah. Melted it up in a spoon and gave himself a shot in the arm. It's the third one today that I know about. He was talking pretty crazy for a few minutes and then he just lay back and passed out." Luder pulled a chair over to the table and sat down, pouring himself a cup of black coffee. "I wish he wasn't in on this," he said. "He makes me nervous."

"He makes me nervous, too," Cribbins said. "But what the hell, we needed him. He had the machine gun; he was willing and able to use it. That's one of the troubles with this kind of caper. You always need a guy like Santino."

"You shouldn't needle him about the girl, Harry," Luder said. "You know how he is."

"I know how he is. But don't worry. The girl doesn't mean a thing to him. He's just mean. Mean and crazy."

"That's what worries me—he's crazy."

Cribbins shrugged. "Don't worry," he said. "I can handle a punk like him any day. Anyway, it'll end in another few days. As soon as Mitty and Goldman show."

Luder lifted the coffee and sipped. His eyes were troubled when he spoke. "There's still the girl upstairs," he said. "What do we do about her, Harry?"

For a moment Cribbins stared straight ahead and said nothing. Then he shook his head and spread his hands out, palms up. "She invited herself in on this," he said. "Nobody asked her. Nobody wanted her."

Luder nodded. "Sure," he said. "But that don't change it—she's here. So what are we going to do?"

"There's only one thing to do," Cribbins said.

Luder looked at him for a long minute and then shook his head. He said, "I don't like it at all."

"We've already knocked off one guy," Cribbins said.

"That was different."

Cribbins reached for the bottle and poured a small shot into the coffee cup. "Look," he said. "I don't like it either. But it isn't a case of liking or not liking. It's one of those things. In this business a lot of things happen that you don't like. A lot of innocent people sometimes get in the way and get hurt. It's tough, but that's the way it is."

Luder still sat there, slowly shaking his head. "She's just a kid, Harry," he said. "Just a kid!"

Cribbins got up suddenly, slamming the cup down on the table.

"God damn it," he said, "go to bed and leave me alone. Just don't think about it. Nothing's happened to her yet. I don't know what is going to happen, but let's let it go for tonight. I've had about all I can take, with that God-damned creep inside and everything else."

Cribbins had two more drinks, sitting alone at the table and staring into space. Finally he looked down at his watch, nodded and stood up. He left the kitchen and entered the living room. He walked very quietly and the dog didn't awaken when he opened the door to the dining room.

Luder lay on one cot, flat on his back, his mouth open and snoring gently. He had loosened his tie and removed his shoes. Across the room, Santino stretched out on the other cot. He lay facing the wall and Cribbins knew that he was dead to the world.

A moment later and he had turned and found the staircase. He removed his shoes before he started to climb to the second floor.

It was the movement of the bed which awakened Joyce. For several seconds she just lay there as consciousness slowly came back, lay in a state of semistupor, trying to put things together and trying to bring her mind into focus. She knew where she was. She was in a bed with a strange girl in an old mansion up in northern Westchester. She was in a bed, and . . .

It was the sound of the heavy breathing and the sudden soft moans which snapped her into complete reality. For a brief moment she thought that the other girl must be having a nightmare. She started to lean over and awaken her, when the realization suddenly struck her. In that brief moment she could feel the blood rush to her head and for a moment then she thought she would faint.

It was a sensation like none she had ever before experienced—a sensation of utter shock and surprise, to be followed a split second later by a terrible feeling of embarrassment and humiliation.

She wanted to cry out in protest, wanted to do anything but just lie there. She closed her eyes tight and held her breath until she thought that her lungs would burst. There was nothing she could do. It went on and on and it seemed it would never stop, and then suddenly the bed was still and the moans were ended and there was nothing but the heavy breathing.

There was the sound of the muffled voices then and

once more the bed creaked and she could tell when he had lifted his weight off of it and got to his feet.

Joyce lay still, scarcely breathing. She felt as though she herself had been ravaged.

Cribbins was halfway down the stairs, walking carefully in his stocking feet in the semidarkness of the early dawn, when he heard the sounds coming from below. He stopped instantly, his hand going instinctively to his left armpit, before he realized he'd left his shoulder holster with the revolver in it down on the kitchen table.

He cursed under his breath and strained his ears to listen. The sounds were coming from the dining room. It was a sort of scuffling noise and then suddenly there was a series of short, sharp barks.

He breathed a sigh of relief, remembering the dog. He went to the kitchen first and strapped on the shoulder holster, but didn't bother with his shoes. Then he moved through the hallway and opened the dining-room door. The first streaks of daylight were penetrating the faded curtains at the tall windows at the end of the room.

Flick was standing straight-legged, straining at his leash and whining. Cribbins took a step into the room and looked over at the cot on which Luder slept. Luder's eyes were open and he was watching him.

"What's wrong with the mutt?" Cribbins asked in a low, irritated voice.

"He wants out," Luder said. "They always have to go out the first thing in the morning."

"Can't he wait?"

"He could," Luder said, "but it might not be so pleasant!"

"All right," Cribbins said, "I'll take him out. I could do with a little fresh air myself."

Luder closed his eyes again as Cribbins crossed the room and untied the dog's leash. Flick began to dance and jump and Cribbins spoke softly to him. He turned and started for the door. He didn't notice that Santino had turned over in his sleep and was no longer facing the wall; he was unaware of the other man's cold narrow eyes on him as he left the room.

Cribbins stopped in the kitchen long enough to put on his shoes. He had to drop the leash and the dog dashed madly around the room.

Cribbins looked up and noticed the rag lying on the chair on which his foot rested. It was a piece of silk with a couple of knots tied in the center, and he remembered that Luder had been using it when he played with the dog the previous evening.

Cribbins reached for the rag and tossed it to Flick. "Here," he said, "for God's sake play with that. Calm down a little, will you, boy? I'll be ready in a second."

Flick had the rag in his mouth a few moments later when the two of them left the house by the side door and walked down the drive toward the old carriage house. They stopped once or twice while Flick investigated some tree trunks, but apparently they failed to suit him and he struggled on, straining at the slender leather lead.

Flick found a post at the side of the carriage house and he stopped, dropping the rag. He circled several times and then finally decided to do what he had to do.

Cribbins drew a sigh of relief as the strain on the leash was taken off and he tucked the end of it under his arm to reach for his cigarettes.

He was in the midst of striking a match when the rabbit leaped out from behind a bush not ten feet away. Cribbins didn't see the rabbit, but his oversight was more than made up for by Flick. The poodle didn't even bother to lower his left hind leg; he took off with one gigantic leap, simultaneously releasing a series of howls.

Although he burned the fingers of his right hand in his attempt to grab the departing lead, Cribbins's efforts were futile. The dog was already a hundred yards away.

Joyce learned of Flick's escape a couple of hours later when Paula brought her downstairs to have breakfast. Paula had gotten up around seven-thirty and although Joyce was awake at the time, she was unable to look at the other girl or speak to her. Once, while Paula was pulling on her clothes, Joyce opened her eyes and she saw that the other girl was watching her covertly. There was an amused, sly look on her face and Joyce quickly closed her eyes again and pretended to be asleep.

When Paula was fully dressed she reached over and shook Joyce lightly.

"Okay, sister," she said. "I know you're awake. If you wanta hit the can you better get up and come with me. The cuffs go back on otherwise."

Joyce sat up, avoiding Paula's eyes. "Thank you," she said in a low voice.

Paula stepped out of the room and returned a moment later and handed Joyce her clothes. "Might as well get dressed," she said.

They went into the bathroom together and washed, Joyce borrowing a comb from Paula in an effort to make herself presentable.

They returned to the room and stayed there until Luder came up and knocked at the door around eight o'clock. "Come on down and get it," Luder said. "Thought I'd give you a break, kid," he continued when Paula opened the door. "Cooked up the breakfast myself. Coffee, eggs, bacon and the works."

The two girls followed him downstairs, and as they reached the landing, they could hear the arguing going on in the kitchen. When Joyce entered the room, Cribbins was seated at the table and Santino was standing over at the stove. The little man gave her a poisonous look.

"Bright," he said. "Real God-damned bright! I told you we shoulda shot that damned dog."

"The dog's gone," Cribbins said. "There's nothing we can do about it. After breakfast, Paula can go out and see if she can round him up. But what the hell does it matter? There's a million dogs around."

"He could go home," Luder said. "It sometimes happens. I remember once . . . "

"That's what I'm telling you. Suppose he does make it back home," Santino said. "Why, Jesus . . . "

Cribbins stood up and stretched. "Yeah, suppose he does? You expect him to tell where he's been? You think he's a talking dog?"

"What happened?" Paula asked. "Did the mutt get away?"

"Shut up and keep out of this," Santino said. He swung around viciously and spit the words out at her. "It's your fault, anyway. The dog shoulda been up in that bedroom last night—not you."

"Lay off her," Cribbins said. "Lay off her, Santino. I've told you . . . "

"Maybe you better lay off her." The little man turned to Cribbins and stared at him coldly. "You think I'm stupid or something? You think I don't know what went on last night, eh?"

He crossed the room suddenly and grabbed Joyce's arm. "He was up there last night wasn't he?" He demanded. "Up there with the two of you. Jesus, he's a real dilly, this boy, now isn't he? One dame isn't enough for him. He has to climb in bed with two of them. Go on," he yelled, pulling Joyce so that she almost stumbled. "Go on—tell us. Which one of you did he have first?"

"Let her go!"

Cribbins moved as he spoke and as he crossed the room he pulled the revolver from the shoulder holster and quickly flipped it in the air so that he was holding the gun by the barrel. He started to raise it over his head.

Quickly Luder jumped between the two men. "Harry, for God's sake!" he said. "What's the matter with you two, anyway? Are you trying to wreck everything?"

Santino jerked Joyce around so that she stood between himself and Cribbins. He held her with one hand, and even in that tense moment she was amazed at the strength in the little man's hands. The hand which wasn't holding her arm had gone to his pocket and in a second he had the switch-blade knife half raised.

For a minute he and Cribbins stared at each other.

"Drop it," Luder said. "Drop it!"

Santino was the first to break. Slowly he lowered his arm, taking his hand away from Joyce while he closed the knife.

"Tell him to lay off me then," he said in a tight voice. "Tell him to lay off me and to keep his paws off of property which don't belong to him."

Paula spoke. "I'm nobody's property," she said. "You might just as well know it now, Santino."

Santino turned and stared at her and then slowly walked over and sat down at the table. "So that's the way it is."

"That's the way it is," Cribbins said.

Luder moved to the stove and picked up the coffee pot. "Oh, let's just have some breakfast," he said.

Santino looked at him and then his twisted mouth opened in a crooked smile.

It was after they had eaten and the men had left the room that Joyce first missed the scarf. She and Paula had finished the dishes and while Paula was again making up her face, Joyce asked if she might have her bag back. She wanted to get her comb out of it. The girl shrugged her shoulders and said sure.

"Except you won't find your wallet," she told Joyce.

She brought the bag in from the front room where it had been tossed and Joyce, going through it, noticed that her scarf was missing. She remembered having taken it with her on Monday morning when she had left the house with Bart, remembered having stuffed it into her bag when she had taken it off the previous evening.

It was odd how the loss of the scarf upset her. Her wallet was gone and so was the cashier's check for twenty-six hundred dollars, but somehow it no longer seemed to matter to her. The scarf was something else again. It had been a present from Bart, the first thing he had ever given her.

It was nothing but a silly little piece of blue and yellow silk, and it probably wasn't worth more than a dollar, but its loss seemed to bring everything that had happened into sharp focus and she had a hard time keeping the tears from her eyes.

Flick's escape from the white house in Cameron Corners may have brought a certain sense of relief to Joyce Sherwood, but it created a definite moral problem for a middle-aged poultry farmer by the name of Corwell Harding.

Harding was a retired mail carrier who a few years back had bought a farm at the edge of the village and he lived mainly on the proceeds of a small pension. He also raised fryers for the market and sold eggs. He was a childless widower and he didn't really need a lot. The eggs and the fryers which he sold to the new supermarket gave him a little extra money and made his life a bit more comfortable.

Things would have been fine for him, if it were not for the weasel. The weasel had started coming around nights, a couple of weeks ago, and within a short time had managed to kill off almost half of his flock of white leghorns, including some of his best layers. It was on Wednesday morning, while he was out checking up on the night marauder's most recent slaughter, that he first saw Flick.

Without hesitancy the dog came when he called him. Harding rubbed the poodle behind the ears and was pleased when the dog put his paws up and looked pleadingly into his eyes. He took the dog inside and fed him, noticing the leash attached to his collar. Harding didn't know a great deal about dogs, but he realized that this was probably a valuable animal. He guessed it had escaped from a passing car. He knew he hadn't seen it around the village before.

Then it occurred to him that a dog around the place might be very good protection. He could leave him loose on a long rope at night near the coops; it might solve the weasel problem.

There was only one trouble. The dog had a rather expensive collar around his neck and he must belong to someone. Harding reached down and examined the collar. He noticed at once the license tag attached to it.

If it wasn't for that license, with its identifying number, he'd be perfectly safe in keeping the animal. Should the owner show up, he could tell the truth and say the dog had just drifted in and he'd given it a home. But the collar was there, with the license tag on it.

Almost subconsciously he undid the buckle, stood up, and walked over to the kitchen cabinet over the stove.

Once more he looked at the tag and then slowly he opened the cabinet and placed the collar on the shelf.

It was something he was going to have to think about. Harding was essentially an honest man, but after all, the dog had just drifted in; he hadn't stolen him.

He opened the icebox, looking for some more meat scraps. He'd have to think this over, but in the meantime, the animal appeared to be famished.

At eight o'clock on Wednesday evening a multicolored hound of mixed ancestry, making his usual nightly rounds of garbage cans in the neighborhood, stopped at the same post in back of the carriage house which Flick had found to be so much to his liking some fourteen hours earlier. The hound immediately performed the same act which Flick had been performing when he'd been disconcerted by the sight of the rabbit. Then the hound leaned down and sniffed and his nose came into contact with the knotted rag which Flick had dropped.

The dog promptly took the rag in his teeth and walked proudly off, passing through the woods in back of the house.

By the time he reached the street running parallel and behind the street on which the Bleeks mansion was situated, he had already grown tired of his new toy and he dropped it and cantered off, looking for new worlds to conquer.

The following morning, a ten-year-old named Charles Wells was bicycling down the street, delivering morning papers, when he spotted the twisted piece of cloth. He stopped and putting up the stand on his vehicle, reached down and picked it up. It took him several minutes to untie the knots and then he spread out the square of blue and yellow silk. It was very pretty. The only trouble was that sharp teeth had torn it so that it was beyond repair.

Young Wells said a naughty word and reconsigned his find to the gutter.

9.

PATROLMAN COOGINS walked into the squad room and squinted his eyes, trying to see through the fog of smoke. Coogins had been needing glasses for years but refused to get them, having the fantastic idea that glasses made a cop look like a sissy.

He finally spotted Sims and went across the room and tapped him on the shoulder. "The boss wants you," he said, when Sims looked up. "Says to meet him in the diner across the street."

The detective nodded and reached into his pocket and held out a handful of cigars.

Coogins examined the bands carefully before putting them into his pocket. "Thank you, Horace, thank you," he said. "These look very nice indeed."

"They should," Sims said. "Old Rumplemyer himself gave them to me."

Coogins nodded sagely.

"That's more than he gave the commissioner," he said. "He's up there with him now, and from the noise he must be raising several new kinds of hell."

"I wouldn't be surprised," Sims said.

He left the room and walked along the corridor to the main door. When he entered the diner he knew just where to look. Detective Lieutenant Martin Parks was seated alone in the last booth.

Sims ordered a ham on rye and a glass of milk from the counter as he passed on his way back. The lieutenant had a cup of black coffee on the table next to a three-decker sandwich which he hadn't touched.

"Sit down, Horace," he said, and when the other man squeezed his big bulk into the booth opposite him, he heaved a long sigh and slowly shook his head. "I just left 'em."

"Things pretty hot?"

"That's too mild a term," Parks said. He picked up the coffee and sipped it for a moment or so and then spoke again. "You know," he said, "my old man was really smart."

Sims looked at him questioningly.

"Yep," Parks said. "My old man was smart. He was a fireman over in White Plains for forty-two years. A plain, ordinary, everyday fireman; not a lieutenant or a captain or a chief, but just a fireman. When he retired he owned his own home, had sent three boys, including me, through college and he didn't owe a dime in this world. He went down to St. Petersburg and bought a small place. My mother died there and so Dad stayed on, playing shuffleboard and fishing. He died last year—he was eighty-seven. Never sick a day in his life, never had an ulcer, never had a worry. He was a smart man. Wanted me to become a fireman just like himself and he told me I was nuts when I said I wanted to join the cops. He was absolutely right."

Detective Sims nodded sagely. "Your old man was smart," he said. He looked up at the other man and smiled. "Jesus, Marty," he said, "you got it bad today. What's the matter? The commissioner eat you out?"

Parks smiled wryly. "The commissioner, the mayor, the chief, as well as old man Rumplemyer, whom I don't have to remind you is more important than any of them in this town. Also the guy from the insurance company, who by some stroke of foul luck happens to be a cousin of the mayor's. Also a few casual gents from the press, and just about everyone else you can think of."

He picked up the sandwich and then put it back on the plate, looking at it with distaste. "It's a funny thing," he said, "but you take a town like New York. Maybe they have six or eight jobs like this Rumplemyer thing every year. In the good years they may solve three or four of them and so they got a fifty-percent average and every one thinks they're doing great. The fact is, of course, that they are. But we get a thing like this maybe once in twenty years. If we solve it, fine; we're only earning our salaries. But if we don't, why then we average off batting zero and, brother, we stink."

"Sure," Sims said. "That's the way these smaller places are. The Rumplemyer thing is a big deal here."

"It's a big deal anywhere," Parks said. "The trouble is, it's the only deal in a town this size."

"Well, being a cop in a place like New York is different," Sims said. "Hell, take the Mad Bomber business. The guy operates for about twenty years, the papers raise hell and so does everybody else. But for twenty years the cops work on it before they finally crack it. No trouble, no squawking, nothing. They're left alone. It's just another thing and sooner or later they break it. But that's New York."

"That's just the point," Parks said. "Something like that happens up here in Brookside, and if we take twenty years to crack it I'd be walking a beat for the last nineteen of those years. It's what I'm saying—up here, excuses don't go. They expect miracles."

The girl stopped at the side of the table and put down the food which Sims had ordered and he waited until she left before he spoke.

"It looks as if it's going to take a miracle to crack this Rumplemyer thing," he said. "What was the upshot of the meeting?"

"The upshot was that the commissioner announced that unless we've done something by the end of the week, he will supersede me and personally take charge. That's what he promised Rumplemyer, and that's what he all but announced to the press."

"That will be great," Sims said. "It's the only break the gang needs to insure a successful getaway."

"Don't be disrespectful," Parks said.

They both laughed.

Parks picked up the sandwich and this time bit into it.

"Okay," he said. "Let's quit horsing around. Let's see exactly where we are and what we've got."

"We've got precious little," Sims said.

"Right. But let's just review what we do have. To begin with, those lab boys that came up from New York have gone over the armored car, the pushcart and the moving van with a fine-tooth comb. Nothing—absolutely nothing. Of course tracing the moving van was simple. Oddly enough, it wasn't hot. It was bought a few days ago from a dealer in New York. The buyer used a phony name and address. We have a description and the dealer has looked over mug shots until he's damned near blind.

"Slagher, the guard in the back of the armored car, was knocked cold when the van crashed into them. He doesn't remember how long he was out, but it doesn't matter. That gas bomb they used took care of the rest of his morning. It damn near took care of him for good.

"There was the milkman who was a couple of blocks away and heard first the crash and then the gunfire. He *would* have to be half blind. The only thing he knows is that there was another car there and that it sped away as he started running toward the accident. Well, I don't need a blind milkman to tell me that. But what kind of car it was, or how many men were in it, he has no idea. And that brings us up to date—except for this mug Mitty."

Sims nodded in agreement. "You think it was the best thing, letting him out," he said. "After all . . ."

Parks spread his hands and shrugged. "We were getting nowhere with him while we held him," he said. "You know how those punch-drunk bums are as well as I do. Sometimes the more stupid they are the more stubborn they are. Holding him was getting us no place. Not, of course, to mention the fact that we would have had to charge him on the robbery if we'd have wanted to keep him and I doubt if we could have made an indictment stick. But the point is, he was no good to us in jail. Now that he's out, we may get someplace—that is, assuming he was mixed up in it."

"He almost has to be—working for Rumplemyer and everything."

"Look, Horace," the lieutenant said. "You've been with it long enough to know nothing is for sure. If he was in on the thing, how do you account for him trying to steal a car within minutes of the stickup? If he was the finger man on the job, he would have been miles away at the time, getting himself an alibi. If he was in on the actual stickup, he'd have left with the rest of the gang. They wouldn't have taken off without him. Hell, it would have been the only sensible thing to do. As you say, he's about all we've got, but he's only good if he's free. That's why

I made it easy for him to get bail on the hot-car charge. We tailed him from the minute he left the jail. Well, he did just about what you would expect him to do. Drove off with the shyster who bailed him out. They went directly to New York and split out.

"The New York Police cooperated with us and they've been using their boys ever since. Both Mitty and the shyster were tailed. The shyster is connected with a mouthpiece named Goldman, a big shot. Real estate operator, sports promoter and a little bit of everything. Shady, but not shady enough to lose his professional standing or ever get into trouble. Goldman represented Mitty once or twice before when he was in trouble, as it was logical that he call him in this time. There's nothing to do as far as Goldman or his assistant is concerned. They acted like lawyers, and that they had a right to do.

"Mitty himself has just been hanging around town. He's made no attempt to get in touch with his lawyers, hasn't seen anyone in particular. He's checked into a flea bag on West Forty-seventh Street near Broadway. The New York boys are staying with him. And that's just about it."

"It seems that *is* it," Sims said.

Parks made a wry face. "Right," he said. "Well, let's get back to the sweat shop. You know," he added, "I wish this was the way it was in those new, realistic detective books where the cops solve the crime with nothing but plain, dull, routine police work. You know, just the boring, steady, consistent monotony of everyday procedure. Police procedure, hell! What we need *is* a miracle."

They stopped at the counter and without discussing it, took coins from their pockets and matched each other. Parks lost and paid up.

They were crossing the street to enter the police station when Sims saw the man entering the building ahead of them. "You've got another headache waiting, Lieutenant," he said. "He just walked into the building. That Sherwood guy. Remember, we talked with him last night. The guy who's wife is missing."

Parks groaned. "I knew it was going to be one of these days. This is what my old man meant, I guess. Maybe she's come home. I can hope, anyway."

"Don't hope, Marty," Sims said. "You know they never bother to let us know if it's good news."

It was the sense of complete helplessness which bothered him most. He'd been in tough spots before—any guy who'd seen active duty had been in tough spots. But this was different. This time he wasn't given the option of doing anything about it.

Bart Sherwood turned over on the bed and looked at the small, square alarm clock on the side table. It was seven o'clock and he pulled himself up, sitting on the edge of the bed. He was beginning to wonder how long a man could go without sleep.

Seven o'clock, Thursday morning. Joyce had been missing for almost three whole days.

It was funny how a house could change. The very sight of their apartment depressed him. The place, without Joyce, was nothing. He would have left and stayed in town except for that chance that she might call. He had to be available. But within the last three days he'd grown to hate the place. The apartment had never been much, but they had been happy in it. Wildly, ecstatically happy, it seemed to him now.

This morning he determined to go through the old routine. He knew that he didn't dare let down the bars, couldn't permit himself to crack up.

When he entered the shower, he turned on the cold water. Afterward he toweled himself and dressed. He took out his best suit and was careful in the selection of a shirt and tie. He was determined to keep up his morale. He started for the garage to let Flick out for his morning run and it wasn't until he was halfway there that he remembered that Flick too was missing. The sudden remembrance brought a lump to his throat.

It was while he was having ham and eggs and coffee in a small restaurant over in town, to which he had walked with the thought that the exercise would be good for him, that he made the decision about the private detective. He'd suggested the idea to the police the night before, but they hadn't been enthusiastic.

"We're doing everything that can be done," they'd told him.

Well, maybe they were, but Bart wasn't going to miss any possible bets.

From the restaurant he walked to the railway station and caught the commuting train he usually took into New York. He got off of the train at Grand Central, but instead of walking up Madison Avenue to his office, he turned south when he left the station and went down to the Advertising Club. He didn't want to face the curious glances of the people in his office.

Entering the club, he found a telephone booth and called Bill Henricks. Henricks was a man he'd known for several years and was connected with the editorial side of an afternoon paper.

It was difficult finding out what he wanted to know without taking the man into his confidence, which his natural sense of reticence prohibited him from doing, but he finally managed to get the idea across.

"All right, Bart," Henricks said after the long and confused conversation. "I can give you a name. But I should warn you. There really is no such animal as a private detective, at least in the sense that the layman who reads paperbacks and mystery stories thinks of one. There are a number of men licensed as such, and the vast majority of them stick to divorce work. Either that or they are credit investigators, or labor spies, or operate in kindred fields. I still say that no private operator can hope to compete with the police if your trouble is a police matter.

"However, if you insist on seeing one, I can give you a name. He's no better or worse than the rest, but at least he's honest. That's the best I can say for him, and more than I can say for some of the others. He won't give you any bum steers. He'll take your money like all the rest of them, but he won't cross you up."

Three-quarters of an hour later, Bart walked into the office of Arthur Gutzman. It was an unimpressive, two-room suite on the fourteenth floor of a rather outdated Forty-sixth Street office building, on the less expensive side of Fifth Avenue. Gutzman was expecting him.

Gutzman, a short, fat man with hooded, sleepy eyes, sat behind an old-fashioned roll-top desk. He wore a baggy tweed suit and a slightly dirty shirt. He looked like a rather impoverished bookkeeper.

He waved Bart to the chair beside the desk.

"My friend Henricks tells me you got problems, Mr. Sherwood," he said. "You want to tell me about them?"

Bart hesitated a moment, not knowing just how to begin.

Gutzman had had plenty of experience with hesitant clients. "You can tell me anything," he said. "It never goes any further. Don't be shy. Nothing surprises me."

"It's about my wife," Bart said. "She's missing. Has been gone since Monday."

"You've reported it to the police?"

"Certainly."

Bart told the man then, as quickly as possible, exactly what had happened. He started with Monday morning and brought the story up to date. Gutzman didn't bother to take notes, but he was very careful to ask for names and addresses and definite times. When Bart finished, he asked a number of questions; how long they had been married, how long they had known each other and about their friends. Finally he took time to light a blackened pipe and then stood up and paced back and forth.

"And why have you come to me, Mr. Sherwood?"

Bart looked at him, puzzled. "Why, because I wanted a private detective to work on the case, and Henricks recommended you," he said.

Gutzman went back and sat at the desk again. He looked at Bart and shrugged his thick shoulders.

"Mr. Sherwood," he said, "doesn't it occur to you that maybe your wife left of her own volition? That maybe she is staying away because she wants to stay away? She did take the money out of the bank, she took the dog and the car with her, she . . . "

"It's utterly impossible," Bart said. "Of course I realize you don't know Mrs. Sherwood and that you don't know me. But you have to take my word for it. She would not have left of her own volition. I've considered it, thought a lot about it. She didn't. I don't think the police themselves believe for a moment that she did. Something has happened to her."

"The check has not been cashed?"

"No. At least up until yesterday afternoon, it hadn't hit the bank."

"And there has been absolutely no trace of Mrs. Sherwood? The police have found out nothing?"

"Nothing. That's why I've come to you. It seems impossible, but the only conclusion I can come to is that she's suffering from amnesia. There is nothing in her medical history to suggest it, but the only other alternative would be that she had an accident of some sort. And if she had, certainly we would have learned about it by now. The car and the dog or something would have turned up."

"Amnesia." Gutzman looked at Bart for a long moment under hooded eyes. "You know," he said, "I want to tell you something about these so-called amnesia cases. I've been hearing about them all my life. I've even worked on half a dozen jobs where the missing person was supposed to have temporarily lost his memory. But do you know something? I've yet to encounter one, or even hear of one, that wasn't a phony. Mind you, I don't say it can't happen and doesn't. All I say is that from my experience they're phony. It almost always turns out that the victim either took off on a drunk, got mixed up with a woman—if it happened to be a man—or absconded with money which didn't belong to him and blew it. Almost always."

"Are you ruling amnesia out, then?"

"No. I wouldn't rule anything out. I can't. But I try to be sensible about it. You don't think there's one chance in a thousand that your wife could just have taken the money and left you. Well, I want to tell you that there isn't one chance in a hundred thousand that she's suffering from amnesia, if what you tell me about her is true."

"Then you think that something did happen to her. That it was an accident of some sort or that someone . . ."

"I could think that, Mr. Sherwood, or to be absolutely frank with you, I could think that she just decided to leave you." He quickly put his hand up as Bart started to protest. "Listen," he said, "about half of my work is tracing missing wives and missing husbands. Nine times out of ten the party who isn't missing and who comes to me is completely surprised by what has happened to him. Just as surprised as you are. How would you feel about wanting me to find your wife if it turns out she has left you—of her own volition?"

"I'd still want to find her."

"Why? So you could get a divorce? So you could get the money back?"

Bart got to his feet, his face white with anger. "You haven't understood me at all," he said. "My wife and I are in love with each other. Joyce wouldn't leave me. Even if she wanted to, which is preposterous, she couldn't have done it this way. There would never be any question of a divorce. She would never have to run away from me. You have to understand that."

The fat man nodded. "I believe you," he said. "But I'll have to tell you this. You're a friend of Henricks and I want you to know the truth. If your wife ran away with someone else, or just plain took the money and left you, I might possibly do you some good. I might be able to find her. In fact, I probably would be able to, sooner or later. But if, as you insist, something has happened to her, an accident or something else, there isn't a thing I can do for you that the police can't do a lot better and a lot faster."

Bart looked at the other man, discouragement written on his face.

"Nothing?"

"Nothing. You can offer rewards for information, you can advertise and so forth. But you don't need me for that. Frankly, I think it would be a waste of money. You say the police think the way you do, that something must have happened to her. Well, believe me, they'll be working on it, doing everything that can be done. There's nothing you yourself can do except possibly keep after them. Cops are pretty busy most of the time and it's a good idea to keep after them on things like this."

He hesitated for a moment and then went on. "I guess those boys out at Brookside where you live have plenty on their minds right now, too," he said. "I remember reading about an armored car stickup out there this week."

"It happened Monday morning," Bart said. "The same day that Joyce disappeared."

Five minutes later he thanked Gutzman for his time and left the office. He decided to call his secretary at the office and then catch a train back to Brookside. He would do the only thing which Gutzman had to suggest—keep after the police.

10.

PAULA brought the newspaper into the house on Friday, shortly before noon. It was a New York paper and had been dropped off at the drugstore.

Cribbins took it from her at once and went over it avidly. He was pleased to see that the Rumplemyer story was buried on the back pages of the second section. It was the usual follow-up story, brief and without information. Police working on the case said they had several leads, but nothing definite had developed so far. A single sentence mentioned that funeral services had been held the previous afternoon for the murdered driver of the armored car.

Cribbins read the article carefully and then dropped the paper to the floor and stood up. "It's time I called Goldman," he said. "Paula, get the car out."

Santino looked up. "Maybe I should go with Paula and make the call," he said.

Cribbins shook his head. "No, you stay here. It doesn't matter if I go out. That old bag across the street saw me when I arrived and thinks I'm Paula's father. She sees me going out for a ride and she won't think nothing of it. You'll be better off here, in case anyone noses around. After all, this is supposed to be your house."

"If it is, I'm getting damned sick of it," Santino said. "Tell Goldman to hurry it up—we gotta get out of here as fast as possible. Anyway, I think this whole Goldman deal is crazy. Why should we sell him the money for seventy cents on the dollar? There isn't one chance in a hundred any of the numbers have been recorded. You know that."

"I don't know nothing," Cribbins said. "I only know we agreed we'd take no chances. Not any. That we'd play it safe. You never can tell about that kind of dough. It came into the brewery from bars and taverns. Maybe, for some crazy reason or another, one of the barkeeps did happen to take down a number. Maybe he thought there might be something funny; maybe he was protecting himself against a stickup. There's just no way of telling.

"So we get seventy on a buck from Goldman and he gives us clean money. We made a getaway, leaving no traces. The only way we can ever get picked up is if the money should be traced. This way, it can't be. We won't even have it."

Santino sat down and frowned. "All right, have it your way. But you're forgetting one little thing. You're forgetting that broad upstairs."

Cribbins stared at him for a moment and then spoke in a soft voice. "I'm not forgetting her—not for a second," he said.

"Then why not let me take care of her right now?" Santino asked. He stood up, starting for the door.

"Jesus, sit down," Cribbins said. "Can't you get it through your head? She was seen coming in here with me. We can't take any chances until we're ready to blow, in case someone comes snooping around. We gotta be able to produce her if we have to. Just take it easy. I'll call Goldman. It can't be more than a couple of days."

Cribbins made his call from a telephone booth in a town several miles away. He was lucky, finding Goldman in and getting through in less than five minutes.

He was very careful. "Did the boy get out of school?" he asked.

"Yeah—he'll be home Tuesday morning. He's got company just now, but he'll get rid of them as soon as he can. He'll be coming into Poughkeepsie on the train and wants to be picked up. Nine-fifteen."

"Shall we plan on you for a visit this weekend?"

There was a long pause and finally the lawyer spoke. "It's rather warm in town," he said. "I hate to travel in this weather."

"It's cool up here. We want to see you. The family may have to leave if you don't come."

Again there was a long pause. "Okay. But the first of the week. Say Tuesday."

Cribbins scowled into the mouthpiece of the receiver. "No later," he said. "We'll have to leave by Tuesday afternoon if you don't show."

Goldman hung up without answering.

Cribbins jammed the receiver on the hook, turned and left the booth.

"Light me a cigarette," he growled at Paula as he climbed back into the car. "I can't handle it with this arm in a sling."

The right sleeve of his jacket was empty, as it had been when he arrived at the house in Cameron Corners. He was taking no chances; he'd arrived there as a man with one arm and he would continue with the subterfuge.

Slouching beside the girl, Cribbins said, "Not till Tuesday. The bastard—you'd think he was doing us a favor."

Paula took her eyes from the road momentarily and stared at Cribbins. "And just what happens Tuesday?"

"Tuesday Goldman comes. By then Mitty will be here, too. We turn the dough over to Goldman and he pays us off. Then we split it up and blow."

She drove on in silence for a few minutes and then spoke

suddenly, her voice bitter. "I'm not going with Santino," she said.

"Nobody says you have to."

"Santino says I do," Paula said.

"Listen, kid," Cribbins said. "The hell with Santino. You do what you want to do."

"Suppose I want to go with you?"

Cribbins reached over and patted her on the thigh. "I like you, Paula," he said. "I guess you know that. But when I leave, I leave alone. It's the way I planned it and the way it's gotta be. I'm not the kind of guy that travels double. Never have and never will. It isn't anything personal—it's just the way I am."

The girl was silent for a long time and then once more spoke, her voice low and husky. "What about me?"

"Like I said," Cribbins said. "You do what you want. If you're worrying about Santino—well, don't. I'll see to it that you cut clean."

"Well, I'll settle for that," Paula said. "I just hope there won't be any trouble with him. You know how he can be."

"I know."

"Another thing," Paula said. "Wasn't it a little risky leaving him there alone with the money? How do you know . . ."

"He's not alone," Cribbins said. "Luder is there with him. The last thing I did before we left was to talk to the old man. He'll be watching him."

"And you can trust Luder?"

"I can trust him. I can also trust him to take care of Santino in case he should get any ideas. Luder is old, but he's been around for a long time. He's sitting back there in the house now with a thirty-eight in his pocket. Santino wouldn't have a chance. The old man doesn't like him and won't need much of an excuse to cut him down to size. Anyway, don't worry about it. Guys like Santino are tough only when they got a machine gun under their arm or are pushing dames around."

Santino made himself a fix a few minutes after Cribbins and Paula left the house. Today, for the first time, his nerves seemed less on edge and he lost the odd jerky movement of his head when he talked. He had shaved and put on fresh clothes and he looked almost human. He sat at the kitchen table and was carefully cleaning his fingernails with the blade of his switch knife as Luder sat across from him reading the newspaper.

"How long you suppose they'll be gone?" Santino asked.

Luder dropped the edge of the newspaper to look over at the other man. He was mildly surprised when Santino spoke to him. Santino very rarely spoke to anyone.

"Oh, an hour, an hour and a half maybe," he said.

Santino nodded. "I ain't been sleeping well," he said. "Last few days, I just can't seem to sleep. I think it's that damned cot in there."

Luder grunted from behind the newspaper. "Yeah," he said. "They aren't soft."

"I'm tired all the time," Santino said. "Always tired!"

"It's that stuff you take," Luder said. "It'll kill you before you're through with it."

"Yeah. Probably," Santino shrugged. "But it's a nice way to die. Anyway, I ain't been feeling good. I got to take something all the time."

He stood up and slowly stretched. "You know," he said, "I think I'll take a little nap. As long as you're going to be down here, I'll go on upstairs. There's a more comfortable bed up there."

Luder dropped the newspaper and stared at the other man.

"You wouldn't be thinking of stopping off at the closet, now, would you?" he said.

Santino looked at him and sneered.

"Oh, sure," he said. "I'm goin' to grab the suitcase and take off. What's the matter with you anyway?" he asked, the sneer turning to a tone of injured innocence. "You think I'm a doublecrosser? You think I'm nuts or something? You're down here. If you don't trust me, sit in the living room. You can see the closet at the head of the stairs from there. You got a gun on you; it ain't any mystery. All I said was I feel tired and I'm going up to find a comfortable bed and get a little shut-eye."

Luder stood up and folded the paper. "Go right ahead," he said. "I'll be sitting in the living room."

Santino followed him out of the kitchen and started up the stairs.

Joyce had been dozing, but the moment the door began to open she sensed it and her eyes flew wide. By now she had become used to their coming and going; she was no longer alarmed when they came into the room. Usually it was Paula, but sometimes old Luder would come up and talk to her. Paula didn't talk a great deal, but just seemed to want another woman for company. Luder, however, liked to talk. He never tired of telling her that he was a "family man" and he talked about animals. She'd grown almost fond of him and preferred his company to that of the girl.

She looked up expectantly as the door gradually opened and then, as Santino stepped softly into the room, she was unable to conceal the sudden disappointment in her face.

He stood at the doorway for a moment, staring at her without expression. Then he turned and carefully closed the door. Joyce felt a shiver go down her spine.

"You and I are going to have a talk," Santino said. He walked across the room and unfolded a camp chair which stood against the wall. Opening it, he pulled it over next to the bed on which Joyce lay.

Joyce pulled the blanket up in an effort to cover herself.

"Yeah, a short talk. You can use a friend, you know."

Joyce nodded, saying nothing. She wondered what was coming next.

"Cribbins has been coming up here," Santino said. "He came up the other night to see Paula. That's right, isn't it? Well, I want to know what they talked about."

Joyce shook her head. "I couldn't tell you," she said. "I was sleeping."

Santino laughed and it wasn't a pleasant laugh. He got up slowly from the chair and took a step so that he was standing over the bed. Leaning down suddenly, he took one end of the blanket and jerked it down.

"You got a pretty face," he said. "Pretty face and a nice body. I can spoil them for you. I can turn that face into something that nobody will ever want to look at again. I can do things to that body of yours . . ."

He stopped then and took the knife out of his pocket. Opening it, he leaned down and almost carelessly drew the naked, razor-edged blade across her breasts.

"Now listen," he said. "Don't play cute with me. Cribbins was up here and you were here. So was Paula. I wanna know what they talked about. They must have talked about something." He smiled at her, his grin evil and leering. "Don't try and tell me you slept through it."

"He was here," Joyce said, her cheeks fiery red. "But honestly, I don't know what they said. They didn't talk."

"Nuts. They talked. Sister, you're going to tell me what they talked about."

His hand reached out and he slapped her hard across the face, back and forth, several times.

"You want me to beat it out of you?" he said. "I'd like to. It would give me a kick. So come on, let's have it. What were they planning? Are they pulling out of here together? Come on, let's have it."

Joyce stared at him, trying to keep the panic out of her eyes. She knew that he wasn't quite sane, wasn't quite human. She would gladly have told him anything that he wanted to know, but she didn't know what to tell him.

"Honestly," she said, "honestly, they didn't talk. If they had, I would tell you."

This time he doubled his fist when he hit her and in spite of herself she cried out. The knife was back in his pocket now and he was sitting on the side of the bed, leaning over her. One hand held her by the throat and the other was balled into a fist to strike again.

"You don't care about your face, do you?" he said.

He was raising his fist then and she struggled and tried to turn her face away. That's when the voice spoke from the door.

"Go ahead, kid," Luder said. "Hit her again. But make it good, because it will be the last time you ever beat a woman."

Santino leaped from the bed and swung around. His hand flashed toward his pocket, but Luder spoke quickly.

"I wouldn't," he said.

"What are you buttin' in for?" Santino said. "What's this to you, anyway?"

"We don't want trouble," Luder said. "I heard her scream. What the hell are you trying to do, raise the whole neighborhood? Haven't you got better sense?"

"I'll see to it that she don't make any noise. Don't worry, I'll see that this bitch is as quiet . . . "

"You'll leave her alone. Hear me? Leave her alone. She's no part of this."

"The hell she isn't. She cut in on this party and she's a big part of it. What the hell do you want we should do—give her a medal?"

"You're a fool, Santino," Luder said. "Hurting her

isn't going to do any good. Just leave her alone and come on back downstairs."

Santino moved a step toward the door and laughed. "You kill me," he said. "A real hero!" He turned to Joyce. "Why don't you tell her we're going to bump her off, hero?"

"I said come on downstairs," Luder said. He saw that Joyce's frightened eyes were on him and he couldn't quite face her. "We haven't decided what we're going to do," he mumbled. "Not yet."

11.

Sylvia Dudbern, Bart Sherwood's secretary, waited until George Swazy returned from lunch before talking to him. She hated to bother him at all, knowing how Mr. Swazy felt about discussing anything which wasn't directly connected with the office. But she felt that she really had to. She'd spoken with Bart around noontime, calling him at his home when he failed to show up for work on Monday morning, and she just had to do something. After all, Bart Sherwood was a member of the office.

Swazy looked up when she came into the room after knocking, giving his usual neutral, rather cold, expectant smile. Swazy was a man who wasted no time on trivialities.

"Yes, Miss Dudbern?"

She was a little pale, realizing that what she was about to do was a bit out of order. But finally she gritted her teeth and spoke, her words rushing out in a tumble.

"It's about Mr. Sherwood," she said. She blushed as Swazy looked at her sharply. "He didn't come in again this morning," she hurried on, "and I had to call him about the Tri-State matter. They . . . "

"I know about the Tri-State matter."

She hesitated a second and continued.

"Mr. Sherwood didn't seem to be very coherent. This thing with Mrs. Sherwood seems to have completely shattered him. He couldn't even tell me when we could expect him. He sounded sick. I just thought that . . . "

"Just what do you want me to do, Miss Dudbern?"

"Well, Mr. Sherwood seemed to feel that the police haven't been making a real effort to find his wife. He's sitting out there in his apartment, all alone, and he just didn't seem right. I thought that maybe if someone here in the office, someone with influence, could just get hold of the police and maybe see what they are doing, and . . ."

Swazy held up a beautifully manicured hand. "They're probably doing everything they can," he said. He hesitated for a moment, looking thoughtful, and then quickly stood up and started pacing the floor.

"All right," he said. "I'll see what I can do. It's a damned shame. Mrs. Sherwood is a nice little woman. Get me the man in the police department who's handling the thing. I'll see what I can find out. We have to have Sherwood back here, and soon," he added.

Five minutes later he had Detective Lieutenant Parks on the wire. It took him a minute or so to make it clear what he was talking about.

The lieutenant didn't pull his punches. "Listen," he said. "Let's get something clear. We're doing everything we can. Everything. It doesn't do one damned bit of good to keep riding us. You better tell that to your Mr. Sherwood. I feel sorry for him, but there's not a damned thing more we can do. "You're Mr. Sherwood's boss, you say?"

Swazy said he was.

"All right. Understand this. The woman is missing, we'll grant you that. But we don't know that anything has happened to her. We don't know that she didn't just go off by herself. And in the meantime, we have other problems. By God, I've got a quarter-million-dollar robbery and a murder on my hands and I'm not getting anywhere with that. Nowhere. A missing woman is important, I'll admit, but we have plenty of other important problems!"

Swazy coughed and interrupted. "Perhaps the FBI . . ." he began.

"They wouldn't be interested, at least not at this stage. They have things to do themselves and there's been no indication that this is a federal case, a kidnaping or anything of the sort. After all, missing wives are a fairly common occurrence. Don't think we're being callous about this, or indifferent. But at this point, until something turns up, there's not another damned thing we can do."

Parks slammed down the receiver and turned to Detective Sims, who had just entered the room "That damned Sherwood thing again," he said. He shrugged his shoulders helplessly. "I feel sorry for Sherwood, but what does he want us to do about it? What does he expect us to do?"

Actually, by this time, Bart Sherwood had given up hope that the police would do anything. That's why he did what he did when he got the telephone message about the dog that evening.

Corwell Harding made his decision over the weekend. It was a difficult decision, but once he made it, he immediately felt better about the whole matter.

He looked the number up in the telephone book on Monday morning and after carefully writing it down, being a methodical man, he made the call.

It took the people at the pound a little longer than he had expected and for a while he experienced a rather forlorn hope that perhaps the record might be lost or misplaced. But it was a futile wish. They called him back around three in the afternoon and told him that the license number of the dog he had given them was for a French poodle and that the dog was owned by a Mr. Bart Sherwood, 97 Olive Drive, in Brookside. Harding thanked them and hung up the receiver. He decided he would write the Sherwoods a letter.

A short time later he brought Flick in from the stake he had him chained to outside of the house and fed him. He had grown very attached to the dog. Watching the poodle as Flick ate his dinner, Harding began to wonder what kind of people owned him. They probably were very attached to him. The chances were that they had children and he could imagine how those children must be feeling about losing the dog.

Mr. Harding began to feel very bad about it. That is why, shortly before nine o'clock that night, as once more he was about to take the dog outside and stake him, he decided that he wouldn't write; he'd telephone them.

He had no difficulty in getting the telephone number from the long-distance operator. He made the call collect.

Bart knew that he should call the police. It was the only sensible thing to do. He was so excited that he had a hard time lighting the cigarette he had instinctively reached for as he started to dial the telephone. And then, suddenly, he put the receiver back on the hook.

The police? What good would that do him. Maybe it wasn't Flick at all. Maybe . . . But of course it was Flick. It had to be; the man was quite sure of the tag number. But even if it was, what would the police do? Nothing.

That's when Bart decided to get a car—rent one if he had to—and drive directly up to Cameron Corners and see the man who had found Flick.

He had to look up the location of the place on the map. He'd been so excited he'd forgotten to ask. Cameron Corners—it wasn't more than an hour and a half at the most. The trouble was the man had been very reticent about seeing him at all that night. He'd said he had the dog and that the dog was in good condition and wouldn't the morning be all right. It seemed he was some sort of farmer and he went to bed early.

Bart had wanted to tell him just how important it was. He started to explain, and then he hadn't been able to go on. How do you explain to a man who has found your dog that your wife is missing? Where do you start?

So he had changed his mind and begged to be allowed to come right up. The man was very reluctant but at last had said he would wait up for a couple of hours. He'd given Bart directions to follow once he got into the town.

It was more difficult than he thought it would be, getting the car. For a moment or so he was tempted to take a cab, but after considering the expense, he made a last try and managed to rent a car from the owner of the gas station he patronized. He was lucky in finding him in when he phoned. As it was, he didn't leave his house until almost ten-thirty.

When he heard the rented car drive up in front of the house, he had a sudden change of heart. He decided to at least call Sims at the police station and let him know what had happened. Detective Sims wasn't in and the man on the desk wasn't sure where he could be reached.

Bart cursed himself for wasting the precious minutes and quickly told the man to leave word for Sims that he had called and that he had a possible lead on his missing wife. He'd call Sims back in the morning. The policeman on the other end of the wire hurriedly asked him something, but Bart was already putting the receiver back.

At twenty to eleven, Lieutenant Parks received the telephone call from State Trooper Ralph Domonitti, stationed at the Hawthorn Barracks.

It was only the sheerest luck that Trooper Domonitti saw the story in the newspaper at all. The paper was a couple of days old, at least, and he was throwing it out with a bundle of old magazines. Usually his wife took care of these chores, but she was in the hospital, nursing the newest addition to his already large family. Right then Trooper Domonitti was home taking care of the other children and doing the housework on his day off. It was only because of his wife's being in the hospital and the attendant problems on his mind that he had failed to read the report on the missing woman which had come into headquarters in the first place.

Seeing the picture of the girl in the paper as he was about to toss it out, brought the thing back to his mind. He recognized her at once and as he hurriedly read the story, he remembered the name and the incident. They'd eat him out at headquarters for not checking the reports, he realized. The only excuse was that newborn baby and it wasn't an excuse the captain was likely to accept.

For a moment Trooper Domonitti experienced a quick temptation; he could just forget the whole thing and say nothing. But as quickly he discarded the idea. He was too honest a cop to ever cover up a thing like this.

So when he saw the picture and recognized the face and then read the story he didn't hesitate to put in the call. He talked with his captain first, verifying the routine flash on the thing, and then he called Brookside. He reached Detective Lieutenant Parks almost at once.

"Last Monday," he explained, "I was on the roadblock just this side of Brewster. Yeah, I'm sure. She showed me her license. It was the Sherwood woman all right. The picture in the paper is unmistakable. Yes, it could have been a French poodle, although I don't know much about dogs. Yes, a black sedan, six or seven years old. Chevy, I believe. And the man with her had one arm. He was average size, around forty or forty-five. Said he was her father and had been ill. She was taking him out for a drive, or at least that's what she told me."

He told Parks he'd write in a full report on the matter. He hung up, wondering what his captain would say to him. He was supposed to check over those reports, and there was no excuse for his not having done so. Well, it probably wasn't too important. If the woman was missing, it was pretty obvious that she wanted to be. He shrugged and went back to his housecleaning.

Lieutenant Parks was completely baffled by the news. It certainly looked as if his first hunch had been right. There was no foul play; the woman had merely picked up and gone off. There must have been another man, after all. Young Sherwood was certainly due for a rather unpleasant surprise.

Still, it was odd that she'd taken no clothes, or returned to the house. He'd tell Sims about it when he saw him the next morning and let Sims break the news to Sherwood.

Corwell Harding gave up around one o'clock in the morning. It was really very inconsiderate; the man had been so insistent, begging him to wait up. And now he'd failed to show. It just went to prove that he'd been silly about the whole thing. He could have saved a lot of trouble and written the letter as he'd wanted to first.

He decided to go to bed and forget the whole thing. As far as he was concerned, he hoped they'd never show up. Before he turned in he once more took Flick, whom he'd been keeping in the house for company, outside and staked him near the coops. It was probably only because he was very tired, that he was a little careless himself.

He tied the long rope to the end of the dog's leash, using a simple slip knot instead of the double knot he usually used. That was why, when he went out to get the dog in the morning, just after daybreak, Flick was no longer there. Nothing was there but the end of the rope.

Harding felt pretty bad about it. Even if he wasn't going to be able to keep the dog himself, it made him feel bad. It was going to be pretty embarrassing if and when those folks showed up.

He had a quick breakfast and then collected his eggs. He delivered them to the supermarket every Tuesday morning around eight o'clock. Before leaving, he scrawled a note and tacked it to the front door. Just said that he had to take his eggs into the market and that he'd be back in a couple of hours. He was really hoping no one would come to read that note.

The first warning Bart Sherwood had was when the engine began missing. It happened a few minutes after he had passed Hawthorne Circle and came at a time he was on a deserted stretch of the parkway. He pushed the gas peddle up and down several times and the engine coughed and almost stopped. Bart cursed and put the car into second gear. A minute or so later the engine gave an odd, gasping noise and stopped altogether. It was shortly before midnight.

Bart climbed out of the car and opened the hood. He had to use his lighter to see anything at all and he knew very little about automobiles in any case. It wouldn't have mattered. The rented car had blown a head gasket.

His first inclination was to start walking. He knew the last gas station he had passed must be at least seven or eight miles down the road, which would mean there wouldn't be another one for at least ten miles in the opposite direction, in which he was traveling. Somewhere off the road, however, there must be a house where he could use a phone.

The night was starless and there was no moon and he hesitated to start walking. There were almost no cars on the road and he realized the futility of hoping anyone would stop this late at night. And yet he felt that he couldn't just stay there and wait. He had to get to Cameron Corners. He tried to be rational about it, tried not to build up too much hope. After all, it wasn't Joyce, it was only the dog. Flick had turned up, and Flick had been with Joyce when she disappeared. It could mean everything or nothing. He was bitter with impatience as he stood by the stalled car and tried to think.

At last he made his decision. Just walking at random would be hopeless. Sooner or later a cruising police car would be bound to pass. He would have to be content to sit and wait. Climbing back into the car, he turned off the headlights. He would conserve his battery, be sure that there was juice so that he could flash a distress signal when he saw a car coming.

It was almost daylight when the trooper stopped. And it was almost eight o'clock when Bart Sherwood finally arrived in Cameron Corners. The garage man whom the trooper had called had lent him a beat-up jeep to use while he made repairs to the rented car.

Bart didn't stop for breakfast, but drove directly out to Harding's chicken farm. He passed Harding's half-ton pickup truck on the way out not, of course, recognizing it.

They had been up since daybreak and she could sense the tension as they sat in the half-dark of the kitchen waiting for breakfast.

Today the routine was changed; instead of Paula's leaving the room they shared and one of the men coming up to guard her, they'd let her come down with the other girl. Heavy drapes had been tacked over the windows of the kitchen and she was unable to see out, but she knew that it was early in the morning.

The thin, wispy one, the dangerous little man with the foul tongue and the nervous, vicious manner, had been steadily cursing under his breath as he paced back and forth. The older one, Luder, sat off to one side, drinking coffee and staring out the window. He seemed morose.

The girl glided about silently, preparing the breakfast and saying nothing. Cribbins didn't come downstairs until later and he was silent and dour. At eight o'clock he finally stood up and stretched.

"It's about time to start in for Mitty," he said. "Santino, you better take the car and meet the train in Poughkeepsie. But get her upstairs first." He nodded over to where Joyce sat finishing her breakfast. "All the way up, this time."

As Luder started to get to his feet, Santino quickly moved across the room.

"I'll take her up," he said. "You finish your breakfast. I'll take her up."

Luder turned a questioning eye to Cribbins and Cribbins nodded.

"Let him do it," he said. He looked back at Santino as the little man reached out and took Joyce by the arm.

"Make it snappy," he said. "I want you to get started for town."

She was unable to control the shiver of revulsion as he grasped her bare arm and propelled her through the doorway and to the staircase. They climbed to the second floor and as she instinctively hesitated in front of the room where they'd been keeping her, he cursed and shoved her.

"Keep goin'," he said.

They walked on to the narrow flight leading up to the third floor.

It was a small, square room, again at the back of the house. There was a frayed rug on the floor, an old-fashioned bed and a high, mahogany wardrobe with its double doors hanging open. Green curtains had been drawn at the windows, which were unshuttered.

"Get on the bed."

She hesitated, sudden fright making her powerless to move. Santino lifted his hand and struck her a sharp blow and Joyce felt the blood hot on her lips. In spite of herself the tears came to her eyes.

She lowered herself, sitting on the edge of the bed.

He struck her again, without warning, and as she fell back, he lifted her feet so that she lay across the bed. He used a thin nylon rope to bind her ankles together, muttering under his breath as he worked. She lay there, staring at him when he ordered her to turn on her side and put her hands behind her back. She didn't move fast enough for him and he punched her with his fist.

He put the gag in her mouth, using a dirty, crumbled handkerchief, after cruelly binding her wrists together.

When he finished he turned her over so that she lay facing up. He stood back and stared down at her, again muttering under his breath. She tried to take her eyes from him, but there was something about the little man that hypnotized her. He was evil—evil and vile and terrible as he stood there watching her.

He started to move, leaning toward her, and at that moment they heard footsteps outside the door. It opened and Cribbins entered the room.

"Damn it, I told you to hurry it up," he said. "You got no time for fooling around now. I want you to go in and get Mitty."

Santino took his eyes from Joyce and looked at the other man. "Why the rush? You sure Mitty will be coming in?"

"Goldman said so. That's as sure as anyone can be. Go and get him."

"And then?"

"And then, damn it, come back here. We'll give Goldman until noon. He'll be driving up. Until noon—that's all."

"And if Mitty ain't on the train?" Santino asked.

Cribbins looked at him blankly. He shrugged. "Come on back."

"Paula could go for him," Santino said.

"I want you to go."

Santino swore under his breath, but left the room, followed by Cribbins, who carefully locked the door from the outside. A few minutes later she heard a car start up somewhere below.

Miss Abernathy was watching out of her living-room window as Santino wheeled out of the driveway. She was getting ready to walk into town and do her weekly shopping at the supermarket.

Back in the kitchen, Luder lighted another of an endless chain of cigarettes and looking over at Paula, he half shook his head. "I don't like it," he said.

Paula didn't answer him.

Upstairs in the small square bedroom Joyce lay tense and still on the bed and stared at the ceiling. They were getting ready to make their getaway. She knew that the time had finally arrived. They were going to play it safe; there were going to be no loose ends. For the first time since that fatal morning, sheer horror came over her.

When Mitty left the hotel on West Forty-seventh Street, he knew he was being followed. He'd been followed every hour of every day since he had returned to New York, and it was beginning to get on his nerves.

Mitty wanted to get up to Cameron Corners. That's where the money was and that's where the others were. Cameron Corners represented safety. He knew that sooner or later he'd be picked up again. That business of getting out on bail had been too easy. The cops weren't that stupid, not even small-town cops like those guys up in Brookside. He knew why they'd made it easy for him; they figured he'd lead them to the others. And if, after a certain length of time, he failed to do so, why they'd just pick him up again and throw him in the can.

Another thing bothered him. How long would they wait for him up there in the hide-out? Just suppose things got a little hot and they had to blow the hide-out and find a new place—what then?

It wasn't that he didn't trust them—that is, it wasn't that he didn't trust Cribbins. Cribbins wouldn't let him down. But suppose Cribbins had to take it on the lam? The thing to do was to get up there and do it as soon as possible.

He could understand why the lawyer had warned him. The man who had come up from Goldman's office had made himself very clear.

"You're not to try and duck out and make your meet until the boss lets you know," he'd said. "You'll have to hang around for a few days until the heat cools off. The chances are ten to one they'll put a tail on you. So don't try to get in touch with us; don't try to get in touch with anybody. We'll keep in touch with you."

That had been several days ago, and still nothing had happened. No one had gotten in touch with him. No one had come near him except the two teams of cops who took turns tailing him.

It was Monday evening, a week from the day they'd pulled the Rumplemyer job, and Mitty was getting worried. He knew that if the police decided to pick him up again for questioning, it might be a lot more difficult to get him out. The cops were always able to hold a man if they really wanted to; they had a million ways of doing it. This was especially true of a man like himself, a man with a record and without important connections.

Walking down Broadway, Mitty took the opportunity at a cross light to turn and look behind him. There were two of them now, the tall, thin one with the blue suit, and the heavy, middle-aged one who always carried a rolled-up newspaper. They were about a block behind him. He could tell; they might as well have been wearing uniforms.

The light changed and Mitty crossed the street and walking another half a block, turned and entered a cafeteria. He'd been coming here every evening for his dinner; it was the place the lawyer had told him to go for his meals.

Mitty went to the counter and found a tray and silverware. He ordered a fish plate and picked up bread and butter and a glass of milk and then took the tray to the front of the cafeteria where he found a table facing the window. Out of the corner of his eye he saw that the tall cop had followed him into the place and had picked up a sandwich and a cup of coffee. He was seated several tables away. Mitty looked out through the window and wasn't surprised to see the other cop seated in a black sedan at the curb in front of the cafeteria.

He was turning back to his food when the man in the open sports shirt walked past the table, hesitated a moment looking around the crowded restaurant, and then turned back and pulled up a chair.

He didn't look at Mitty as he took the food off of his tray and put it down. When the tray was empty, he leaned over to place it on one of the unused seats. Then he spoke. His lips barely moved and his voice didn't carry more than a few inches, but Mitty heard him.

"Tomorrow morning," he said. "The seven-fifteen to Poughkeepsie. You'll be met."

Mitty coughed, covering his mouth. He didn't look at the other man.

Sitting down, his companion reached for the sugar and again his words reached Mitty. This time Mitty was looking directly at him, but he saw no movement of his lips at all.

"There are two of them on you," he said. "One outside in a car, one a few tables away. Have you made them? Don't speak, just take out a cigarette if you have."

Mitty reached for a cigarette.

"Dump them tonight. Hit an all-night movie and get that train in the morning. But be absolutely sure you've gotten rid of them. Don't take any chances."

Ten minutes later Mitty got up and left the cafeteria. He walked to the corner of Forty-third Street and found a cab at the stand. He climbed into the back and closed the door.

"South on Seventh Avenue," he told the driver. "I'll tell you when to stop."

As the cab pulled away from the curb, he turned and looked behind. The sedan was following. There were two men in the front seat.

Mitty had to laugh. Two cops. Well, it made it a little more complicated, but still they'd be a cinch. The first thing to do was to cut it down so the odds would be a little more even.

Mitty leaned forward on the seat and held two single dollar bills in his hand.

"When you get to Fourteenth Street," he said, "cross if you have the lights and then slow down on the other side. Just enough so I can jump out quick."

The driver looked at him in the rear-vision mirror curiously, then reached a hand back for the money.

"Okay," he said. "It's your neck, bud."

The lights were right and the cab driver crossed Fourteenth. Just past the intersection, he braked and pulled toward the sidewalk. Mitty had the door open and was out of the cab before the car came to a stop. He ducked into the subway kiosk and ran down the steps. Putting a token into the turnstile, he walked out onto the platform. In the distance he heard the rumble of an approaching train.

Risking a look, he saw that the taller of the two detectives had just entered the station. The man pressed through the turnstile and stood on the platform several yards away. Mitty knew that his partner would stay with the car until he heard from the other man.

When the train came in, Mitty climbed aboard. The doors closed and the train started south. Mitty knew that the thin man was at the other end of the car.

They both got off at Houston Street station. Mitty walked over to a coin machine and inserted a nickel, fumbling with the machine and shaking it. He was killing time until the two or three persons on the platform left. A minute or so later he strolled down the platform and entered the men's room. It took him only a second or two to reach into his pocket and take out the handful of quarters which he twisted up in the handkerchief. Then he went back to the platform.

The tall, thin detective was waiting a few feet from the entrance. Instead of avoiding him and going toward the exit, Mitty suddenly swung around and walked directly toward him. The man was watching him curiously as he approached. Mitty had a cigarette in his mouth.

"Say, mister," Mitty said, "you got a match?"

The detective stared at him coldly and half turned away. "No smoking in the subway," he said.

"No?" Mitty said. He reached up to take the cigarette from his mouth with the hand which concealed the tightly rolled up quarters. "That's a shame," he said, and as he spoke his hand suddenly lashed out.

Mitty could hear the click of the coins as the blow struck the side of the detective's head. The handkerchief split open and the quarters fell to the cement floor. The thin man also fell and Mitty caught him with an uppercut as he was halfway down.

He turned and walked casually to the exit. Passing the change taker's booth, he looked into the startled eyes of the clerk on duty.

"The son of a bitch made an indecent proposal to me," he said.

Twenty minutes later and he'd found an all-night theater.

12.

THE SENSIBLE THING would have been to wait. The man was bound to return sooner or later. But Bart Sherwood found it impossible to just sit there and do nothing. He had read the note on the door, checked his watch.

Harding apparently lived alone, as there was no sign of anyone about the place. The dog, however, should be around. It wouldn't be likely the man would take him to town with him.

It went against his grain to do it, but Bart stepped off the porch and rounded the corner of the house. He looked in through an unshaded window. There was nothing and so he walked back and looked into the kitchen through a second window. Then he whistled and called Flick's name. If Flick had barked in answer he would have waited. But there was no sign of the animal and so he climbed into the car. Twenty minutes later he was back in Cameron Corners.

A quick drive down the main street convinced him the logical place for Harding to sell his eggs would be the supermarket. He parked the car and entered. Corwell Harding was leaving the manager's office, pocketing his wallet, as Sherwood stopped at the cashier's cage and put his question. The cashier pointed the man out and Bart quickly crossed the almost empty store.

"Mr. Harding?"

Harding looked up, opened his mouth to answer and then stammered, suddenly at a loss for words. He knew at once that this must be the man whom he'd telephoned about the dog.

It took a little time for Bart to explain why he had been delayed and then more time for Harding to tell him about the dog. He was embarrassed about it. And this man, Sherwood, couldn't quite seem to get it through his head that the dog had once more escaped. He seemed utterly baffled, totally crestfallen by the news.

They walked to the front of the store as Bart continued to question him.

"He just wandered in," Harding said. "Like I told you, last Wednesday it was. No, I'd never seen the dog before. Have no idea where he could have come from. He looked all right, not hurt or anything. Except he was pretty near famished."

"And now he's gone again," Bart said, his voice helpless and tired. "Gone."

Harding nodded. "I'm sorry," he began, "but . . ."

"Maybe someone around has seen him. I can advertise . . ."

Harding shook his head. "No paper here," he said. "But he certainly couldn't have gone far, not in just these last few hours. Now, if you were to just sort of drive around and ask." He hesitated, looking past Bart's shoulder. Suddenly he touched the edge of his hat and bowed.

"Morning, Miss Abernathy."

He half turned and Bart turned with him.

Bertha Abernathy stopped and dropped her shopping bag to the floor. "How are you, Corwell," she said.

Harding said he was fine. "Say, Miss Abernathy," he said, looking up sharply. "You haven't by any chance seen a dog running around loose? A black French poodle. This here gentleman . . ."

Miss Abernathy looked up at the ceiling and thought for a moment. She turned to Bart when she spoke.

"The fact is, I did, only a short time ago," she said. "It was right after I left the house. The reason I noticed him, he was wearing a collar and there was a short leash attached to it. Only I don't think it could be this man's dog."

"No?"

"No. I think it belonged to those folks who rented the old Bleeks house, across the street from me. Brown's their name. They're new. Anyway, last Monday Mrs. Brown's father came to visit her—with his own nurse, if you please —and the nurse had a black French poodle. I think that was the dog I saw this morning. It looked like the same dog that showed up at the Bleeks place on Monday."

Bart Sherwood looked at her sharply. "You say the dog first showed up here on Monday."

"That's right, young man. On Monday."

Fifteen minutes later Bart Sherwood drew up in front of the old Bleeks house and parked the car. For a moment he just sat there and stared at the house.

It was probably completely ridiculous. He wondered just what he would say, what he could say. There probably wasn't even the remotest connection between the dog who belonged to the woman who'd been renting this house and his own dog. On the other hand, Flick had definitely been in Cameron Corners. Flick had disappeared the very day this other poodle had arrived in the town. It could mean nothing, or it could mean . . .

He was still thinking about it, wondering just what to do, when his eye caught the movement at the window.

It was a small thing, the mere quick dropping of a curtain as someone stepped away from the window inside of the room. But there was something oddly secretive about it. Someone had been watching him, someone who didn't want to be seen.

Quickly he got out of the car. That strange, surreptitious movement had been enough to decide him.

He had to wait several minutes before his knock was answered.

"I've got this fellow Sherwood on the outside wire," the desk sergeant said over the intercom. "He wants Sims and Sims isn't in so I thought I'd see if you wanted to talk to him. He seems a little excited, Lieutenant."

Detective Lieutenant Parks jerked erect in his chair.

"You're damned right I want to speak to him," he said. "We've been trying to reach him for hours. Put him on." He grabbed for the outside phone and waiting only to be sure that the connection was made, spoke quickly, before Sherwood had a chance to say anything.

"Where the hell have you been?" he yelled. "We've been trying to get hold of you. Something has . . . "

Bart quickly cut in.

"I'm up in a place called Cameron Corners," he said. "Got here early this morning. Someone reported finding Flick—that's the poodle who was with Mrs. Sherwood when . . . "

"You found the dog?" The lieutenant's voice was excited.

"No—no, that is to say he was found and then he got

lost again before I got here. But I ran into something else. Something that seems a little queer. It probably doesn't mean anything, but I think I should tell you about it."

For the next several minutes he talked to the lieutenant, explaining about Harding's call. He told about his trouble in getting to Cameron Corners and his delay. Then he told the officer about meeting Miss Abernathy and going out to the Bleeks house to see the Browns.

"But when a girl answered the door, she denied that they owned a poodle, or a dog of any kind. She seemed odd, almost frightened. That's when the man came to the door."

"What man?"

"I guess it must have been her father," Sherwood said. "This Miss Abernathy said her father was visiting her. Anyway, he was a one-armed man and he . . . "

"A one-armed man?" The lieutenant almost yelled the words. "You say a one-armed man?"

"That's right. A middle-aged man with one arm, and he ordered her . . ."

Once more the lieutenant cut in. He made an effort to control his voice, to be very sure that Sherwood understood him.

"Quick, where are you now?"

"Why at the drugstore in town . . ."

"Stay right there. Don't go anywhere, don't say anything to anyone. Stay there. We'll be up in less than an hour. Just don't move."

He was half out of his chair while the receiver was still crackling as Bart yelled into the mouthpiece some forty or fifty miles away. . . .

The lieutenant knew something. There was no doubt about it. He had some piece of vital information. He hadn't told Bart; had cut the connection while he was trying to question him. But he'd been excited and he'd been very definite about Bart's staying there and waiting for him.

It had to be something to do with that house. Something to do with the sulky, uncommunicative girl who had answered the door and denied knowing anything about a French poodle. Something to do with that ill-tempered man with one arm who had ordered her away from the door and then crossed the room to slam it in his face.

Those two knew something. The French poodle had

been Flick. And Flick had been in that old colonial mansion.

Joyce had been in that house. Suddenly he knew it. Knew that she had been there and that perhaps she was still there.

He paled as he turned and left the drugstore. If Joyce was there, she would be in terrible danger, because right now they would be growing suspicious.

Lieutenant Parks could not possibly arrive before another hour, not even with the help of sirens and a motorcycle escort. Bart Sherwood ran for the car he'd left sitting in front of the drugstore.

He didn't make the turn which would have put him on the street which passed the house. Instead he went an extra block and then circled, so that he came upon the place from the rear.

This block was lined on both sides by woods, and the woods separated the street from the rear of the old white house. He pulled the car into the curb and parked. As he stepped to the ground he noticed the rag lying in the gutter. He only saw it for a fraction of a second out of the corner of his eye, but that fraction was enough. At once he recognized the tiny square of yellow and blue silk. Reaching down, he picked up the torn scarf.

There was no question about it, no question at all. It was Joyce's scarf, the scarf he had given her. His face blanched and for a moment he just stood there, torn by conflicting emotions.

Joyce had been here. There was no doubt of it. He could almost feel the closeness of her. But then, as his fingers caressed the torn and ragged piece of silk, he felt a cold chill come over him. He had to get into that house, at once.

It wasn't difficult to find cover as he crept toward the place. He was crouching, not thirty feet from the back door, when the car turned into the drive and stopped at the side of the house under the carriage porch. Two men, a thin, bitter-mouthed little man in a sharkskin suit, and a bulky, wide-shouldered man with the broken face of a prizefighter, got out of the car and entered by the side door.

He waited only a minute or two and then he crept forward again, staying half concealed by a high hedge. Gradually he made his way to the place where he had noticed the small window which apparently opened into a cellar.

Cribbins waited only until Mitty and Santino were in the house and had closed the door.

"We're leaving," he said. "At once. We can't wait for Goldman."

"What's up? Hell, I just got here." Mitty looked baffled as he tugged at his cap.

"No time to talk," Cribbins said. "But that damned dog disappeared, and a few minutes ago some guy was around asking about a French poodle. He knew the dog had been here. I don't know who he was or what he wanted but it doesn't matter. We've got to blow. We can't take any chances; can't hang around here any longer."

"I thought you said we had to wait for Goldman," Santino said, his voice sarcastic. "Thought it was important to . . ."

"Do anything you want," Cribbins said. "I'm blowing now. We can get in touch with Goldman later on, but I'm getting out now."

Luder, standing at one side of the room, spoke up.

"I'll go with you," he said.

Cribbins hesitated a moment. "I'm going alone," he said at last, speaking softly. "We got plenty of transportation; you and Mitty and Santino can take one car . . ."

Santino interrupted. "You're all worrying about nothing," he said. "As far as I'm concerned, I stay here and wait for Goldman. He'll be here in another hour or so. You guys want to get out, go ahead." He looked over at Cribbins. "And I suppose the girl's going to be my problem, once you take off?"

Cribbins stared at him for a moment and then spoke slowly. "Either way," he said. "Either way. I'll do it, or you handle it."

Santino laughed. "Forget it," he said. "I just wanted to know how you felt about it. But the pleasure's mine. That way, I'll be sure."

"I know that," Cribbins said. "You like this sort of thing. So go on upstairs and handle it. I'll get the money." He reached down to the suitcase which he'd brought from the upstairs closet and unlocked it, lifting up the top. "Your cut will be here when you get back."

The four of them—Cribbins, Luder, Mitty and Paula—watched silently as Santino slowly walked toward the door, passed through and carefully closed it after himself. They could hear his footsteps as he mounted the stairs. . . .

The small, bitter-faced man passed within less than three feet of him as Bart crouched behind the door leading from the cellar into the hallway.

He'd been there for less than a minute, but the voice had reached him through the crack in the door. He'd fought desperately to kick his shoes off and now, as the man passed and started up the stairs, he slipped noiselessly through the doorway and followed.

He didn't know who else might be in the house, up on one of those floors, waiting, but it was a chance he had to take. Following, crouching down and creeping up the carpeted steps, Bart Sherwood silently thanked God for the hard months of basic training he'd taken as a Marine while he was learning jungle fighting.

They reached the second floor, first the little man and then Bart, a moment later. They continued on up to the third floor.

His ears told him what his eyes were unable to see, as he waited at the edge of the staircase. The man had passed down the hallway a short distance. He could hear the key as it was inserted into the lock of the door.

Bart stretched the twisted sock he held, one end in each hand. He straightened up and moved swiftly.

Joyce Sherwood heard the key in the door and she struggled and turned on her side so that she was able to see, in the dim light of the shaded room, the door as it slowly opened. Her eyes widened and she tried to scream through the gag which bound the lower part of her face. The light coming through the crack between the drawn blinds and the window caught the right edge of the knife blade.

Again she tried to scream and her body writhed on the bed and then her eyes closed tightly and she waited in paralyzed horror. A split second later she opened them wide as she became aware of a sudden commotion, the grunting and then the tortured sound of quick, sharp-drawn breaths.

She saw him then, in the dim light—saw Bart and saw the little man struggling against the twisted cloth tightening around his thin, stringy neck.

She thought her eyes were lying to her, and she fainted.

"He's been gone for more than ten minutes," Cribbins said, his voice tight. "What's keeping him, anyway."

Paula looked over at him and her voice was bitter when

she spoke. "Can't you guess? Why don't you go up and see?"

Cribbins glared at her. "Go up and get him, Luder," Cribbins cried.

"Let Mitty go. It's out of my line." Luder turned away and crossed over to the window. "Let's get out of here. Right now. I got a funny feeling . . ."

Mitty humped his huge shoulders and stood up. "Where's this room?" he asked.

"Third floor, second to the left when you get to the top of the stairs."

"It will be all right with me if you take care of Santino too," Paula said.

Mitty left the room without a word.

Bart stood just within the door, one hand holding Joyce as she stood behind him. He held Santino's knife in his other hand. His words were a whisper when he spoke.

"Someone's coming," he said. "Get back. Get behind the bed and stay there."

"Oh God, Bart!" Joyce said. "Oh God, they've got guns and . . ."

"Do what I say. Give me room."

She crept back then, walking half blindly.

Mitty took his hand from the knob and stepped back, a look of dumb surprise on his face. Then suddenly he laughed.

"All right, Santino," he called. "All right. You had your fun, now come on. The boss says we're leaving."

He waited a moment then and the smile on his face changed into a frown. He lifted a huge fist and rapped on the oak panel of the door.

"I said come on!"

Twice more he banged on the door, and then he cursed and turned and went back to the head of the staircase. His voice was an outraged bellow as he called down.

"He won't lemme in. He's in there with the girl an' he won't open up or even answer me."

Inside the room, Bart quickly turned to Joyce.

"They're coming up the stairs, all of them," he said in a whisper. "We've got to get out of here!"

Joyce looked at him with a helpless expression as he moved to the window. He jerked the cord of the shade and it flew up. When the window failed to open, he lifted his foot and kicked out the glass. Looking down, he saw the flagged courtyard three stories below.

Then there was a pounding at the door and Cribbins's voice called out. "Come on, Santino, open up!"

The command was followed by sudden silence. Bart's eyes went to his watch. It was exactly twenty minutes since he'd made his call to Parks. He felt the sense of utter helplessness come over him. The detective couldn't possibly arrive before another half hour.

He leaned down with his ear to the crack of the door, hearing the whispering outside.

"I say leave," Luder said. "Now. The hell with him. Leave him in there with her if he wants to stay."

Cribbins spoke in a hurried whisper.

"No! There's something wrong. Something has happened. The girl is still inside. We have to be sure. We can't go without being sure. Mitty, break down the door."

Bart no longer worried about being quiet. He rushed across the room and grabbed the heavy wardrobe, dragging it to the door. He spoke as he moved.

"Get at the window," he told Joyce. "I'm going to hold them as long as I can. Get at the window and get ready to jump. Hang by your hands and bend your legs a little as you drop."

She stood staring at him, and he had to yell at her again. She nodded dumbly, and at that moment there was a shattering crash as Mitty threw himself against the locked door.

"Bart," she said, "Oh Bart! I can't. I . . ."

Then the sound of the siren reached their ears, coming up from the street below them.

Bart fell to the floor, yelling for Joyce to lie down as he did so. A second later a stream of bullets splintered through the panels of the door, followed by the confused noise of footsteps as those outside started for the staircase.

There was a dead silence then for a full minute.

The staccato bark of the riot gun reached his ears as Bart knelt, a couple of feet from Santino's body, holding Joyce in his arms as sobs wracked her slender body.

Coincidence had State Trooper Domonitti on routine patrol just north of Brewster when the message came over the intercom. He was driving the interceptor, a Ford with a souped-up Merc engine and rear end, and he was accompanied by a fellow officer, which was unusual, since he nearly always drove alone. The message itself was relayed from the Hawthorn Barracks and was rather vague. Merely a standby order at an address up in Cameron Corners; they were to see that no one left the house until the arrival of the Brookside police.

Domonitti used a heavy foot on the throttle. It wasn't, however, until he hit the business district of Cameron Corners that he found it necessary to use his siren in order to get through the midday shopping traffic. There wasn't much traffic, but Domonitti was in a hurry and he didn't want to slow down until he reached his destination. He was still worrying about his momentary lapse in the matter of that missing girl, and he was anxious to make a good showing.

Domonitti had no reason to connect the message with that lapse—no reason at all until he pulled into the driveway and leaped to the ground after hearing the shots coming from the house, and then ran toward the front porch and saw the door open and the face of the one-armed man he had questioned at the road block a week previously. He recognized the face without difficulty. The only thing was that now the man no longer had a single arm. He had two arms, and in them was cradled a submachine gun.

It was Mitty who, inadvertently, saved Domonitti's life. Mitty was directly behind Cribbins, and he was carrying the suitcase with the money in it.

Cribbins, seeing the state police car and the troopers, was raising the gun. His finger was pressing the trigger when Mitty crashed into him. It spoiled Cribbins's aim and gave Trooper Domonitti the fraction of a second he needed to lift his service revolver and fire. Domonitti aimed by sheer instinct and he was lucky. The first two shots took Cribbins in the chest and he stumbled, falling to one knee and dropping the machine gun.

The trooper who had been accompanying Domonitti was already out of the police car and had taken the riot gun from behind the rear seat. The sight of the machine gun was all he needed. As Mitty swerved to avoid Cribbins's fallen body, Luder and Paula rushed out of the door behind him. Luder had a .45 in his hand and Mitty was reaching for the gun he had shoved down into the band of his trousers.

The trooper released a burst of fire from the riot gun.

Of the three of them, Paula, Mitty and Luder, Mitty was the lucky one. He was stumbling over Cribbins, so the stream of lead missed him. Luder took a single bullet in the face and was dead before his body hit the ground. Paula was hit three times and although she was seriously wounded, she'd live.

The suitcase containing the money slipped from Mitty's hand as he fell and broke open as it rolled down the porch steps and struck the gravel driveway.

The quarter-million dollars taken from the armored car made a rather impressive sight lying there in the midday sun.

It was well after three o'clock now, and they'd been sitting there, at trooper headquarters in Hawthorne, for the better part of an hour. Lieutenant Parks finally stood up and reached for his hat.

"Well," he said. "I guess that's that. It's a lucky thing I called the state troopers. I'd never have made it in time."

He turned to where Bart sat, his arm around Joyce.

"And neither would they," he said, "if you hadn't followed your hunch and broken into that house. But I guess everything is all right now. There'll probably be some kind of a reward for cleaning up the Rumplemyer job. You should certainly be in on it." He smiled. "You'll be able to get that new car for your husband—and then some, Mrs. Sherwood," he said.

Joyce looked up at him, her face still pale but her eyes sparkling.

"We're going to get Flick back first," she said. "If it takes every cent we have, we're going to find him."

Bart's arm tightened around his wife. "Finding a missing dog should be simple," he said. "Simple—compared to finding a missing wife."